The Stars That Shine

By Julie Clay

Illustrated by Dan Andreasen

BASED ON STORIES TOLD BY AMERICA'S BIGGEST COUNTRY MUSIC STARS

Vince Gill, George Jones, Brenda Lee, Patty Loveless, Loretta Lynn, Tim McGraw, Willie Nelson, Dolly Parton, LeAnn Rimes, Marty Stuart, Pam Tillis, and Trisha Yearwood

Simon & Schuster Books for Young Readers

NEW YORK LONDON TORONTO SYDNEY SINGAPORE

SIMON & SCHUSTER BOOKS FOR YOUNG READERS
An imprint of Simon & Schuster Children's Publishing Division
1230 Avenue of the Americas, New York, New York 10020
Text copyright © 2000 by Julie Clay
Illustrations copyright © 2000 by Dan Andreasen
All rights reserved including the right of reproduction
in whole or in part in any form.
SIMON & SCHUSTER BOOKS FOR YOUNG READERS
is a trademark of Simon & Schuster.
Book design by Paul Zakris
The text of this book is set in 13-point Berkeley Oldstyle.
The illustrations are rendered in oil paint.
Printed and bound in the United States of America
2 4 6 8 10 9 7 5 3 1

LIBRARY OF CONGRESS CATALOGING-IN-PUBLICATION DATA

The stars that shine / by Julie Clay ; illustrated by Dan Andreasen
p. cm.
"Based on stories told to her [i.e. Julie Clay] by America's biggest country music
stars: Vince Gill, George Jones, Brenda Lee, Patty Loveless, Loretta Lynn, Tim
McGraw, Willie Nelson, Dolly Parton, LeAnn Rimes, Marty Stuart, Pam Tillis, and
Trisha Yearwood."
"To create awareness for St. Jude Children's Research Hospital."
Summary: A collection of stories about childhood and growing up,
using a variety of settings.
ISBN 0-689-82202-2
1. Children's stories, American. [1. Short stories.] I. Clay, Julie.
II. Andreasen, Dan, ill.
PZ5. S7967 2000   [Fic]—dc21
99-086465

Lyrics on page 45 are from "Coat of Many Colors" by Dolly Parton.
Used with permission of Velvet Apple Music © 1998.
J-200 guitar model depicted on the cover supplied by

Page 101 constitutes an extension of this copyright page.

The author has donated 10 percent of her advance proceeds to St. Jude Children's
Research Hospital and has developed companion products and events to
further promote the hospital.

To Taylor

Acknowledgments

Thanks to Simon & Schuster for embracing the heartfelt idea behind this collection and letting it blossom into a wonderful working relationship. In turn, St. Jude Children's Research Hospital proved to be a receptive and grateful partner, and every one of the country music artists threw themselves into the mission with their customary enthusiasm and generosity. A simple thank-you would never be enough. I found out quickly that they are truly "stars that shine."

And in the end, thanks to my daughter for giving me the initial inspiration to write, to my husband for his unfailing belief in my abilities, and to my mother for her tireless assistance on this project. Without them, this book would not have been possible.

Ingram 11/00

Contents

Preface

"Mother, tell me a story again about when I was little," my daughter would ask as she hopped on my lap. The sweet request—made almost daily—never failed to make me smile, because of course, she was still very little.

So, I'd begin recalling her favorites: the day she was born; the time she fell and had to have stitches; stories about me when I was a little girl. One after another . . . on and on . . . happy and sad and funny, they were family memories brought to life with many "made-up" details here and there.

"Tell me what happened next, Mother," she would interject at the slightest pause in the storytelling. And so, I'd continue until we'd both decided on a good stopping place, but not before we'd sung for a moment together. The songs were usually nothing more than little ditties half remembered—some famous, some made up, many passed down—but all performed with much bravado. And as exhausting sometimes as my daughter's appetite was for these story-and-song sessions, I sadly knew that there would come a day soon when she wouldn't want to hear stories, when she wouldn't want to have sing-alongs. When would that be?

And then one day not too very long ago, I answered my own question when I was visiting with my mother. "Mother," I said, "do you remember the story about when I got so homesick at sleep-away camp? How did it go?"

Well, of course I knew exactly how it went, but she always told it so much better, and in true showstopping style, she launched into the telling as I lovingly savored every word as if it were the first time I had ever heard it. And likewise, she delighted as much in the telling as I did in the listening.

It was then that I knew: My daughter would never tire of the stories and the songs, just as I hadn't, just as my mother hadn't. And I realized, too, that many of the best stories have never been written. Stories where we are the main characters. Stories that are homespun. Personal stories that are from the heart.

It was from this revelation that *The Stars That Shine* naturally evolved. And as a result, I offer this collection as a celebration of story and song. They are stories inspired by some quite well-known people of song that most likely would never have been invented. They are personal memories and family stories based in remembered detail that I've "fictionalized" along the way. They are new stories that I hope the reader will choose to take as his or her own. Stories to pass down and around. Stories designed for children—the child in all of us.

Julie Clay
NASHVILLE, TENNESSEE

A Letter from St. Jude Children's Research Hospital

St. Jude Children's Research Hospital was founded by the late entertainer Danny Thomas. As a struggling young actor during the depression, Danny prayed to Saint Jude Thaddeus, the patron saint of hopeless causes, and asked the saint to "show me the way in life." In return, Danny made a promise to one day build a shrine to the saint.

After Danny found success as an actor and comedian, he dreamed of a hospital where sick children could come for treatment—regardless of race, religion, or a family's ability to pay. He sought to establish an institution where doctors could treat children with life-threatening illnesses, while scientists could conduct research that would ultimately lead to cures. When St. Jude Children's Research Hospital opened its doors in 1962, Danny's promise had become a reality.

Today, Danny's "little hospital in Memphis" is one of the premier biomedical research and treatment facilities in the world. In just thirty-six years, St. Jude's has treated more than fifteen thousand children from across the United States and around the world. St. Jude's played a key role in increasing the survival rate of acute lymphoblastic leukemia, the most common form of pediatric cancer, from less than 4 percent to more than 80 percent. The hospital continues to make advances in innovative treatments such as bone marrow transplants and cell and gene therapy.

Country music has played an important part in St. Jude's mission. Country Cares for St. Jude Kids is one of the most successful radio fund-raising events in America. These two-day "radiothons" are broadcast from more than 160 radio stations nationwide, and more than 100 of the biggest names in country music have participated. Since Country Cares began in 1989, it has raised over $106 million in pledges for the children of St. Jude Hospital.

With *The Stars That Shine,* we at St. Jude's are thrilled to see our friendship with country music grow even stronger. When Danny Thomas prayed to Saint Jude Thaddeus, little did he know that one day some of the greatest entertainers in the world would help him fulfill his promise. We thank Julie and all of the stars involved for supporting the children of St. Jude Children's Research Hospital with these wonderful stories, and for helping us to continue to fulfill Danny's promise.

Richard C. Shadyac, National Executive Director
MEMPHIS, TENNESSEE

Booger Red

A tiny bumblebee had just saved Butch's life, and much to the amazement of the crowd gathered, Butch jumped right over the fence and headed for home. But even if bumblebees could be heroes, this particular bumblebee wasn't the real hero. Booger Red had actually saved Butch, but no one in Abbott except Mama would ever know. It's a long story, but trust me, it'll all turn out in the end.

WILLIE NELSON

The town of Abbott, Texas, was home to about five hundred people then, including the cats and dogs, so saying it was a small town was an understatement. Riding through on your way to Hillsboro or Waco, you could close your eyes for a minute and be far on the other side without ever knowing that Abbott existed. Main Street was not just the main street. Matter of fact, it was the only street, consisting of three whole blocks. And within those three blocks was everything the town had to offer its humble farming population. There was a barbershop, a post office, a general store, a gas station, a blacksmith shop, two churches, a school, and a cotton gin. You could either ring up the telephone operator, Miss Russell, and she'd connect you to who or what you needed, or like most people, you could just walk. From one corner of Abbott to the other—any which way you went—took no more than ten minutes on foot. Or, if you were Booger Red, you'd just ride your cow.

Booger Red wasn't his real name, of course. His real name was Hugh. He was red-headed and freckle-faced, and that partly accounted for the "Red" part. The "Booger" part was because his nose ran and bled awful one time all over his weekly Sunday meeting suit. So, Mr. Fritz, who owned the general store, nicknamed him that, and it stuck. It was okay with Hugh, though. He'd often hang out at the store and drink a soda water, and he had always liked Mr. Fritz.

Booger Red's granddad died when he was only six. Until then, both his grandparents helped raise him and his sister, Bobbie. Nobody much knew about his parents. They had never been around. But it hadn't mattered a bit. Booger Red's grandparents were the only family he had ever had, and they were without a doubt the best mama and daddy in the world.

Years ago, Mama and Daddy had lived right across from the gin, but now Mama lived down a ways in a small house with no electricity and cardboard-papered walls to keep the Texas wind out. She didn't have any farming land. The house just sat on a small lot. Nevertheless, she kept hogs and chickens and a milk cow that Daddy had ridden from time to time. Daddy had been a blacksmith by trade, and he had had a little shop in town where he repaired farm machinery. Or, he would shoe horses and mules here and there for a little extra money.

There was just enough to survive with never a bit to spare, so Daddy's death had left his family in the middle of hard times. It was up to Mama to keep the family going, and thankfully, she was a resourceful and talented woman. During the day, she single-handedly manned the tiny lunchroom at the elementary school, which was a good thing for Booger Red because he always knew her food was going to be good. And then she'd come home and sit at the piano by the light of a kerosene lamp and study her lessons.

Mama had taken piano through the mail from the Chicago Musical Institute for a long, long time. When Daddy got her the piano, it had seemed a frivolous thing for someone trying to make ends meet. But Mama said it was good for her soul. And she was right. Her money from cooking work and the inner peace she found in the keys of that piano were what got them through the hard times. And Booger Red had always helped in any way that he could.

The most money he ever made was raising calves for the Future Farmers of America—best known as the FFA. The way it worked was that you'd buy a calf—your "project," they called it—and fatten it up for a year and then take it to the stock show to sell. If you'd done a good job raising your project, you'd be able to sell it for a high price at the auction. Plus, the FFA would give out ribbons and prize money for the best calves.

Booger Red's past projects had won ribbon after ribbon and had sold for good amounts of money. But last year, his family hadn't been able to scrape together enough money to buy a calf and keep it up, and this year, things hadn't looked any different. Money was short, and suitable work for an eleven-year-old was hard to come by.

"Don't worry, Mama," Booger Red said. "I can always run errands for a nickel or a dime, or I can shine shoes in the barbershop. There're lots of farmers who need helping, too. I can help pull corn or pick cotton."

"That's hard work for such a little boy," his mama said, sighing.

"It's not so bad if you know how to do it," Booger Red said. "You just pick for a while and sit on your sack for a while, then your back and fingers don't ache quite as bad."

"Bless you, Booger Red. But promise me that you'll try to have a little fun. We'll make it somehow. We always have," Mama said as she hugged him tightly.

★　★　★

So Booger Red worked hard and played hard, too. He would go swimming in Blair Creek, or squirrel and rabbit hunting down on Cobb Creek. Or he would fight bumblebees; that was Booger Red's favorite.

Nobody could remember how the game was invented or why, but it was an Abbott Sunday tradition, and Booger Red was the leader of the pack.

"I've found a nest right here in the ground. Get your weapons, men," he'd call to all the other boys gathered in the fields on Sunday afternoons.

Then, everyone would start running and swatting, armed with paddles that they'd made from the boards of apple crates. The game was to see how many bees they could kill without getting stung. But no matter how hard they fought, everybody got stung plenty of times. Some Sundays, Booger Red would come home with both eyes swollen shut.

"Good gracious alive, Booger Red, won't you ever learn? Just look at those eyes," Mama would say as she put chewing tobacco on them to draw the poison out.

The stings were like badges of courage to Booger Red, so he didn't care. The following Sunday, he would proudly head straight back out to battle. He'd never missed a bumblebee fight yet.

One Sunday afternoon, however, a warrior friend named Morris came armed with his paddle weapon and knocked on Booger Red's door. "Where have you been? We're all just standing and waiting in the field. Are you coming or not?" he said.

"I can't go battle bumblebees today," Booger Red said. "I have to wait on the man from the FFA. He's comin' with my calf."

"Thought you couldn't afford a calf this year," Morris said.

"Can't," Booger Red replied matter-of-factly. "But they talked to Mama and said they were going to give me one. 'Cause we're poor, I guess, but Mama says it's 'cause I'm so good at it. Either way, it don't much matter. They're delivering it to us this afternoon."

And Booger Red couldn't wait. He'd missed getting the ribbons, and he knew Mama missed the money from selling the calves, even though she had never said so. One thing's for sure: It beat pulling corn or picking cotton.

The FFA representative pulled up just as Morris was leaving. Mama was standing on the front porch in her housedress and apron, and the man went over and talked to her kinda low for a few minutes. Then he sauntered over to Booger Red. "Well, cowboy, I gotcha a fine calf in here," he said, slapping the back gate of his trailer. "Yep. One of the finest we got this year. Can't hardly go wrong with this one, plus they say you do a pretty good job. That right?"

"Yessir," Booger Red replied, just waiting to see his new calf.

"Well, then," the man continued. "Help me get him out, and he's all yours for a while."

As the man opened the gate, Booger Red saw the prettiest weaning calf he'd ever seen in his entire life. Mama was even admiring the calf from afar and nodding approvingly. Once Booger Red had a little rope secured around its neck, the man hopped into his truck and drove off, yelling, "Good luck. See ya at the stock show."

Booger Red was sure to win with this project, and it would mean the biggest ribbon ever and a lot of money for sure. "We're gonna make a great team, me and you," he whispered in the calf's ear. "And I think I'll call you something big and strong. I'll call you Butch."

From that day on, Booger Red tended to Butch so much that Mama said he was going to spoil him. "You know not to get too attached," she warned.

But this time, Booger Red couldn't help it. Unlike any of his other projects, Butch became Booger Red's pet. Mama would swear that calf knew just what Booger Red was saying. And not only that, Butch did other things that weren't at all normal. Of all things, he acted just like a dog.

Now, it may seem hard to think about a cow acting like a dog, but Booger Red had taught him early on. From the first day, when Booger Red would go out to pet and feed him, he'd pick up Butch by his two front legs and put his hoofs up on his shoulders. So after several times of doing that, Butch would come running up to Booger Red in the mornings and jump up on him like a dog. It was the craziest thing, and of course it got even crazier the bigger and fatter Butch got. Then, like a bullfighter, Booger Red would know what was coming, and he'd lightly step out of Butch's way and say, "Not anymore, Butch. You're too big." And Butch understood and never jumped up again. He was a smart cow. He was Booger Red's friend.

Word spread about what a fine cow Booger Red had raised. So, as the stock show grew nearer, farmer after farmer would come by to see Butch and figure if they wanted to bid on him or not. But Booger Red had decided a long time ago that he wasn't going to sell Butch.

He didn't care about any old ribbon or any amount of money. All he cared about was keeping Butch, and he told Mama so.

"Booger Red, listen to me now," Mama said. "You are selling that cow. We've spent too much time and money feeding and raising him. You don't keep fattening cows. They're for selling and eating. And he's a fine one, too. I'm just glad you had enough sense to stop him from jumping up. Nobody would have paid a cent for a crazy cow, no matter how fine he looked. They'd assume he was rabid for sure," she finished. And that gave Booger Red an idea.

He knew that Butch wouldn't jump up anymore—he hadn't for a long time—at least not without a little help. So on Sunday afternoon, before the big stock show that evening, Booger Red went to the first bumblebee fight he'd been to in weeks. And fighting like crazy, he managed to capture alive one of the biggest bumblebees he had ever seen. It had been a battle, but he had won. With one swollen eye and a killer bumblebee in a Mason jar, Booger Red rushed to take Butch to the show.

The stockyard was overly crowded that night, largely as a result of Booger Red's fine entry. Everybody was congratulating him and predicting he'd win the grand prize.

"Yep," Booger Red said. "I think this year I'm getting the best prize of all."

So when it was Butch's turn on the auction block, Booger Red was right beside him. "Now, Butch," he whispered, "this is our only chance, and it will only sting a little."

With that, Booger Red released the bumblebee right in Butch's ear. Well, you've never seen such a commotion. Butch went wild, knocking over the auctioneer's podium, charging through the stands, on and on and on.

"Get that mad cow outa here before it kills somebody," the auctioneer screamed from under the platform where he was hiding.

But nobody had to wrestle Butch. In one leap, he was over the fence and headed home with Booger Red right behind him. Needless to say, Booger Red hadn't given anyone a chance to bid on Butch, and there was no ribbon awarded to the "wild" entry.

But some things are just more important than others, even if they don't make sense. And after a good tongue-lashing, Mama let Booger Red keep the "good-for-nothin' cow," as she called it. "Why, we can't even get milk from him," she reminded Booger Red.

But she had been the only one to see Booger Red send the bumblebee on its mission of mercy, and she understood. After all, Daddy had bought her a "good-for-nothin' piano" a long time ago. Certainly not something that would put food on the table in bad times. But, like Butch, it was good for the soul.

And Butch did end up being good for something. Booger Red rode him around everywhere, just like a horse. And, of course, Butch could always double as a dog.

✶　✶　✶

Willie Hugh "Booger Red" Nelson continues to enjoy a long-lasting musical career with more than one hundred albums to his credit. Raised in Abbott, Texas, by his grandparents, Willie went to Nashville in the 1960s to pursue his dream of a singing career. He was rejected as a performer but enjoyed success as a songwriter. Some of Willie's classics that were recorded at that time included "Crazy" by Patsy Cline, "Night Life" by Ray Price, and "Pretty Paper" by Roy Orbison.

Eventually, Willie returned to Austin, Texas, and finally had his first big breakthrough as a performer. The 1975 single "Blue Eyes Crying in the Rain" made him a singing success, and from there on, Willie was without a doubt one of country music's biggest stars, with hits such as "On the Road Again," "My Heroes Have Always Been Cowboys," "Always on My Mind," and "Whiskey River."

In addition, Willie has established himself as a film actor, appearing in such films as *The Electric Horseman, Honeysuckle Rose,* and *Wag the Dog,* to name a few. He helped establish the Farm Aid organization, which hosts a massive annual star-studded concert to raise money for American farmers in need. He is also a member of the Country Music Hall of Fame.

Willie talks fondly of his childhood experiences in Abbott, saying he rode a cow long before he ever rode a horse. He was actively involved in the Future Farmers of America and remembers one of his cows, named Butch, who used to jump up on him like a dog. His granddad died when Willie was six, and his grandmother raised him and his sister, Bobbie, primarily by working in the school cafeteria and giving music lessons at her home—a talent she learned by taking lessons through the mail from the Chicago Musical Institute. Best of all, the bumblebee fights were actually an Abbott Sunday tradition—a tradition that Willie thoroughly enjoyed.

Up and Down

PAM TILLIS

Pamela and Harriet were walking down the school hall, talking excitedly about the upcoming contest.

"Yours will most definitely be the best one there," Harriet predicted.

"You really think so?" asked Pamela.

"I know so," Harriet said enthusiastically.

"You sure I can't talk you into entering, too?" Pamela asked.

"No thanks again," Harriet said. "You know contests make me nervous. Not to mention what Bradley Parks may have up his sleeve."

"I think you're just scared that I'll beat you," Pamela teased.

"Think whatever you want. I guess we'll never know," Harriet teased back as they arrived at the lunchroom door.

Each year, there was a May Day celebration for their school, consisting of a picnic held on the neighborhood church grounds. All the students and their families would gather to celebrate the warm, windy spring weather while they ate and played various games. Plus, there was the annual kite-flying contest open to any and all interested students. Near the afternoon close of the festivities, everybody would gather round to watch the kites flying in the breeze, and the teachers were assigned to vote on the best May Day kite, based on design and performance. Then, the school principal would recognize the winner and officially bestow the #1 Flying Ace Award. It was a grand affair, and Pamela was on her way to the lunchroom to enter with Harriet by her side.

As they hurried eagerly toward the sign-up table in the lunchroom, neither of them noticed Bradley Parks stick his big tennis shoe out into the aisle in order to trip Harriet. He

was the class bully, and Harriet was an easy target. No one knew much about her, except Pamela. Harriet was a new student at the school that year, and she was shy.

Whoosh! Harriet's legs flew out from under her, and she landed hard on the shiny linoleum floor. All the students turned to look, and laughed. It was about the tenth time that spring that Bradley had purposely tripped her. "Going somewhere?" he teased as Harriet was scrambling to get up.

"As a matter of fact, we are," Pamela said. "We're on our way to sign up for the contest."

Harriet couldn't believe what she was hearing.

"It'll be hard to fly a kite while you're falling down," one of Bradley's followers laughed.

"Leave her alone," Pamela insisted. "She's not clumsy, and you know it. Just wait and see. Harriet's going to win the contest and show you all."

Now Harriet really couldn't believe what she was hearing.

"What? Are you going to make it for her?" someone asked.

"Of course not," Pamela huffed. "Harriet is perfectly capable of making it herself."

Pamela grabbed Harriet, and they strode to the front of the lunchroom, both officially entered the contest, and left the room.

Pamela lived next door to Harriet on Revere Place, a pretty, tree-lined street with quaint brick houses. There was always somebody to play with, particularly with Pamela's big family and the Jackson family on the other side. Unlike Harriet, who was an only child, Pamela was the oldest of four sisters and one brother. So in and of themselves, they always had enough players for a good game of freeze tag on the big church playground that sat right on the corner. Or if you didn't feel like tag or a pickup game of softball with the Jackson kids, there were monkey bars and swing sets and seesaws and even a big tree house. That's where most all the kids stayed in the afternoon. But this afternoon, Pamela and Harriet went straight up to Pamela's room after school.

"I still can't believe you did that," Harriet said.

"Did what?" Pamela asked. "I just did what you should have done a long time ago. Those kids tease you just because they don't know you, and just because they've been able to get away with it."

"Pamela, give it up. I'll never be as popular as you. Let's face it," Harriet concluded.

And Pamela *was* popular. She was a good student, a talented artist, and had just won the Perfect Penmanship Award for the fourth year in a row. And besides that, she could play the guitar and sing. But she was a bit shy, too, so not many people knew that. She mainly just played and sang for herself and Harriet.

Surprisingly, Harriet was much the same, minus the school popularity—thanks to Bradley Parks. She was tall for her age and extremely skinny, just like Pamela. Harriet was more shy, but she was also a good singer and a good artist. All that made them the perfect friends.

"Come on, Harriet," Pamela urged. "We'll fix it. Let's get to work."

"Okay, but promise me that you'll be there," Harriet said.

"Be there? I wouldn't miss it for the world. We're best friends. Plus, I'm going to beat you hands down," Pamela said, smiling.

★　★　★

Now, the making of kites for the contest had always been a top secret affair. No one discussed their design, much less let anyone see their creation before May Day. Of course, Pamela and Harriet had already decided to work on theirs together, so Pamela posted a DO NOT DISTURB! TOP SECRET! sign on her bedroom door. Sonny Boy was the only one allowed to enter. He was Pamela's younger brother, and since he didn't go to their school yet, it didn't matter if he saw the kites. He was good for fetching Cokes and snacks, little-brother chores that didn't bother him in the least. Getting to work on a top secret project with his big sister was an honor indeed. Plus, he'd always liked Harriet. She reminded him of Pamela.

Day after day, right up until the afternoon before the May Day celebration, Harriet and Pamela worked on their kites. Finally they were finished. Both kites were made of different-colored construction paper and painted with tempera paint. Pamela drew colorful fish on hers, and Harriet chose to depict beautiful swans. The tails were made of matching colored material, and Harriet had added an extra one on hers for good luck. It was hard to pick between the two just sitting there—both kites were creatively designed. The final choice between the two would have to be made on which one flew the best, and tomorrow was supposed to be a sunny, windy day.

As Harriet left to go home, Pamela offered to keep the kites under wraps in her room

and take them for a final, secret test flight at the next-door church playground once everyone had gone home. Harriet agreed. After all, Pamela had brought her this far, and Harriet was grateful.

"See you tomorrow," Harriet called as she walked across Pamela's front yard.

"Can't wait," Pamela said, waving good-bye.

Looking down at the beautiful kites, Pamela could just imagine soaring with Harriet atop the world.

"Did you finish?" Sonny Boy asked as he stood in the doorway to Pamela's room.

"All except one thing," Pamela answered. "When everyone clears out in a little while, I'm going to take them for a test run at the playground."

"You can't do that," Sonny Boy protested. "There's not any wind today."

But Pamela wouldn't listen. She had promised Harriet that she would test the kites a final time, and a promise was a promise.

After Sonny Boy and her sisters had gone off to the school softball game, Pamela ventured out to the church playground with the kites. Sonny Boy was right. There really wasn't any wind, but she wasn't going to let a minor detail like that stop her. She had to make sure the kites were ready. Pamela figured that if she could run fast enough—and she could run pretty fast—and if she picked up enough speed, then the kites would at least rise up on the wind that she stirred behind her.

Pamela tried hers first and, believe it or not, she managed to pull it off. Running as fast as she could, a brief breeze happened to blow over. It was just enough to get the kite above her head.

"That's a winner," Pamela said aloud as she took her kite and set it out of the way by the monkey bars. Now for Harriet's.

Pamela started running again, with Harriet's kite bobbing up and down off the ground. *I've almost done it again,* she thought. *And now, if I could run just a little bit faster, then I could definitely get her kite to soar higher.*

But the only thing soaring was Pamela's unstoppable determination. There was absolutely no wind this time. Running full steam ahead, she'd look back and see Harriet's kite dip and then take off again. And so Pamela ran even faster each time, looking behind her all the while until she turned and came face-to-face with the monkey bars—nose first. Down came her hopes, down came Harriet's kite in a shambles, and *smoosh* went her own kite that was resting beside the monkey bars.

Her nose was hurting really bad. It was broken. And all the painful way home, and then across town to the doctor, Pamela knew that her kite-flying days were over, at least for the time being. But she didn't feel sorry for herself. She felt sorry for Harriet. It didn't matter about her kite, because there was no way she herself could fly it in the contest now. But Harriet's kite was wrecked, too. The contest was tomorrow, she had ruined everything, and it wasn't long before everybody got word of the mishap, including Harriet. Sitting wounded in her room and feeling the weight of Harriet's disappointment, Pamela had to do something. And there was one tiny hope that remained among the wreckage: It was Sonny Boy.

With bandages all over her nose, it was almost impossible to understand what Pamela was saying. Plus, her body ached with pain. She felt terrible inside and out. There wouldn't be enough time to make a new kite, and even if there were, she wouldn't be of any help. So Pamela asked Sonny Boy to repair Harriet's broken one and accompany her to the contest. It was a tall order, but since he had been there while the kites were being made, Sonny Boy had confidence. He accepted the challenge bravely. "Don't worry, Pamela. It will be all right. It's Sonny Boy to the rescue," he said.

It just has to be all right, Pamela prayed as she drifted off to a hard night's sleep.

★ ★ ★

The next day was torture for Pamela. All the kids went off to school, and later they would go to the May Day celebration. Sonny Boy had worked most of the night, but Pamela hadn't gotten to see the repaired kite. Her mother wouldn't allow anyone to disturb Pamela's needed rest.

Sonny Boy flashed Pamela an okay sign as he scurried across the front yard on the way to school. Pamela was left alone, and having the entire day to herself in bed, she began to conjure up the worst possible outcomes. *None of this would have happened if it hadn't been for me,* Pamela brooded over and over again. And by the afternoon, she was in a frenzied state of worry—convinced that Harriet's dreams were certain to come crashing down in front of everybody.

Harriet felt the same way. She was in no shape to help repair her kite. All day, she had sat in school with her head down, and now at home sitting in her room, she had convinced herself that the worst hadn't happened yet. That's why Sonny Boy was having such a hard time getting her to come out. "Hurry up," he called from outside her window. "It's gonna be okay."

"I can't. Pamela and I had a deal. We were going to go together," Harriet yelled back.

"Just think of me as Pamela," Sonny Boy said as convincingly as he possibly could. "It'll be like she's there, because she can see right out her window. And besides, she's counting on you, and she's getting sicker by the minute just thinking about what happened. You have to do it for her," he pleaded.

Thinking of Pamela and all of her attempts to help—even if they hadn't turned out too well—Harriet reluctantly agreed. And clambering down to meet Sonny Boy, she realized that she had made the right decision. Standing outside her front door, Sonny Boy was smiling and holding the kite. A perfectly repaired kite, just for her. Off to the contest they flew.

"Look out the window," everybody was yelling to Pamela from outside. But Pamela wasn't looking. She was scared to look. She could only hope that Sonny Boy had been able to fix everything. "Look out the window," everybody kept calling. So finally, taking a deep breath, Pamela parted the curtains a tiny bit. Staring in disbelief, she parted them some more and then some more.

There was a huge crowd of happy onlookers sitting on the church lawn and staring above. In the center of all the kids who had entered was Harriet. The swan kite was floating easily, high above all the rest, and standing below was Harriet, looking straight up with Sonny Boy close by. As if she could feel Pamela's admiration, Harriet turned toward the window and flashed the most beautiful smile. She was indeed soaring atop the world. Even Bradley Parks couldn't deny it.

"I did it, didn't I?" Harriet asked as she and Sonny Boy bounced into Pamela's room hugging the #1 Flying Ace Award. And following behind were all the neighborhood kids with the biggest bag of popcorn ever for Pamela.

"I sure did fix it, didn't I?" Pamela mumbled through her bandages.

"You sure did. Thank you," Harriet replied.

"No, I mean I really fixed it this time. Now Bradley Parks really knows who the clumsy one is," Pamela said.

Harriet and Pamela hugged each other and laughed.

★ ★ ★

Pam "Pamela" Tillis was born and raised in Nashville, Tennessee, the daughter of singing star and Country Music Hall of Fame songwriter Mel Tillis.

Her big hit in 1991, "Don't Tell Me What to Do," was the first of many, many more hit songs and million-selling albums that are still going strong. Success didn't come automatically, though. Pam made her debut on the Grand Ole Opry stage at age eight, singing "Tom Dooley." And from there she worked steadily for more than ten years as a backup vocalist, jingle singer, club performer, songwriter, and publishing company "demo" singer—all before she was finally recognized nationally. But the talent and determination never left her side, and now Pam reigns as one of the most beloved and respected performers today.

This story revolves around a particularly funny incident that Pam recalls. Growing up on Revere Place, in a suburb of Nashville called Donelson, she lived next door to the Jackson family as well as next to a neighborhood church on the corner, complete with a playground. She was one of four sisters and called her only brother Sonny Boy. A shy, straight-A student with perfect penmanship, Pam did in fact work diligently to make a kite on one occasion, only to try flying it without any wind and break her nose bumping into the monkey bars. Ultimately, Pam's wit and her ability to laugh at herself are what captivate most everyone she meets.

The Ghost of Bayou Bleu

TIM McGRAW

One day, Timbo and Mike were fishing in the bayou and searching for sunken treasure when suddenly Timbo said, "I'm tired of playing pirate games."

"There's nothing better to do," Mike said, shrugging.

"Sure there is. There always has been," Timbo said with a mischievous look in his eyes.

"What are you thinking?" Mike asked, grinning.

"I dare you to go on a real adventure," Timbo challenged. "I dare you to camp out on the island overnight."

Mike didn't flinch. "I double dare you," he said. "I double dare you to camp out on the island overnight on the night of a full moon. That is, if you aren't scared of the ghost of old Bleu."

"You've got a deal." Timbo grinned. And with that they took a solemn oath of secrecy and went about getting ready for their big adventure.

On the surface, it was hard to believe that Mike and Timbo had anything in common. Mike was mousy and shy, on the short side, and skinny as a stick. In almost comical contrast, Timbo was talkative, tall for his age, and the star player on the baseball team. Yet despite the obvious physical differences, Mike and Timbo could have been long-lost brothers. They both had the same mischievous glint in their eyes, and they both loved the bayou. They could be found seven days a week floating around and fishing in those waters, telling everyone about all of their pirate adventures far away on the Seven Seas. They could sail for miles and miles looking for treasure and be back in time for dinner.

Timbo's house was one of the first ones built on the bayou in Start, Louisiana, and it had been right in the middle of a huge cotton field. With cotton almost as far as you could see on three sides, it had appeared as if a mighty blizzard had completely snowed the house in. But over the years, other houses had been built in the field, until it was somewhat of a neighborhood now. Most all of the cotton had melted away into the ancient bayou that ran, hidden, right in back of Timbo's house.

Just a few quick leaps out his back screen door there was a little dock with an aluminum canoe attached, restlessly bobbing back and forth in the murky waters. Then, just across the way, there was an island. You could have rowed out to it in no time, but it wouldn't have mattered. It was a forbidden island. There were alligators that lay under the water right around all the banks—or so the parents said. They were scared to death of what could happen, so all the kids had been threatened with the whippings of their lives if they ever got close.

But Timbo and Mike didn't believe it. They had never gone close enough to the island to be sure, but they'd been most everywhere else around the bayou and had never seen one single alligator. "Oh, they're there, all right," all the grown-ups would warn. "And besides, if they don't get you, Bleu surely will."

Everybody had a story about Bleu, but Timbo always told it best. On the weekends, he and Mike would stay up late at night and tell ghost stories. Timbo would lower his voice and, in a whisper, he would tell the story of Bleu.

"As the story goes," Timbo would begin, "long ago there was a man named Bleu. He was an old fisherman who didn't like anybody or anything. Kept mostly to himself; people figured the alligators were his only friends. And he was as mean as an alligator, too. Day after day, you could catch a glimpse of him on his flat wooden raft. He had a long, crooked stick for an oar that he'd poke down into the muddy bottom, and he'd slowly push his way up and down the waters on the back side of the island. A monstrous sight, he had long fingernails and a hunched-over back, and you could barely see his evil, beady eyes peering out from under the wide brim of his tattered felt hat. And they say that if you got too close to him or the island, he would open his mouth wide like one of the alligators, revealing a row of pointy, scraggly teeth that could chop you to bits in one bite. He was a crazy old hermit who was better left alone. And that wasn't a problem. The alligators would always be enough to keep visitors away."

Timbo would pause, and then continue, whispering low. "One night, though, there came a huge storm that went on through the next day and the next. The cotton fields were supposedly flooded that year, and all kinds of fallen trees and debris were picked up by the swirling waters and washed down the bayou. After the storm finally ended its downpour of destruction, somebody noticed Bleu's flat wooden raft broken into pieces and hung up in a bunch of the floating brush. Downriver a ways, somebody else found his old floppy felt hat. People were certain that he had been swept under during the storm and drowned, because nobody ever saw Bleu again. He was never found. But that wasn't the strangest thing: Every time there was a full moon, somebody would vow that they had seen a fire burning on the island and heard an awful moaning and hissing echoing in the wind. They said the ghost of Bleu had come back to haunt the island and anyone who ever came near."

As Timbo finished the story, there would always be an eerie moment of silence, and then he and Mike would laugh and laugh. Even though it was a great ghost story, neither one of them believed a word of it. They weren't scared. Pirates weren't scared of anything. And that's why Mike had double dared Timbo to camp out on the island overnight.

Timbo ran and got his dog-eared *Farmers' Almanac,* and sure enough, there was a full moon scheduled for Thursday night. So that's when they'd do it. The only catch was that they would have to make up something to tell their parents.

After thinking for a moment, Mike came up with the perfect plan. He could tell his parents that he was spending the night with Timbo, and Timbo could tell his mother that he was spending the night with Mike. They would never get caught.

★　★　★

Timbo woke up very early on Thursday morning but didn't get out of bed right away. He had never gotten up on time, and his mother would surely suspect that something was up if he did. So he just lay there and waited for a while.

Soon, his mother yelled for him. "Hurry up, Timbo, or we're all gonna be late again."

Timbo jumped out of bed, quickly dressed, and ran to the kitchen. As he sat down to eat his breakfast with his two younger sisters, Timbo hoped this would be one day that his mother didn't ask him many questions. No such luck. "And so, Timbo. What's your schedule after school today?" she asked.

Now, Timbo had never told a story to his mother, but she for sure would never let him even go out to the island, much less camp out overnight. But a dare was a dare. And a double dare, too. Plus, he figured that what she didn't know wouldn't hurt her. She'd never know the difference.

"Oh, yeah," Timbo said as if he were just remembering something. "I forgot to ask you. Mike invited me to spend the night with him tonight, and I already said I could."

"On a school night?" his mother shot back. "I don't think that's a good idea. You'll just have to go another time."

"No, I can't," Timbo said too quickly and too loudly.

"And why not?" she asked with one eyebrow raised.

Now Timbo was really in a fix. His mother normally never cared if he spent the night with Mike, but in his excitement, Timbo had forgotten that Thursday was a school night. He'd just have to embellish the story a bit.

"I asked you why not, Timbo," his mother pressed.

"Well, uh, our paper, of course. We have to work on our paper for the short story contest at school."

"The writing contest? Since when did you enter the writing contest?" she asked, surprised.

"Don't you remember, Mom? I told you last week," Timbo continued. "It's a group project, and Mike and I are writing ours together."

"Well, my goodness, Timbo. I've never seen you so excited over a school project," she said, "and I certainly wouldn't want to be the reason why you don't win."

Timbo couldn't believe it. His story had worked. So before she could change her mind, he said, "Mom, you're going to be late." And with that, everybody grabbed their things and ran out the door.

Timbo got to school just as the second bell was ringing, and Mike shot him a worried glance from across the room. He figured something had gone awry. But Timbo quickly flashed the A-OK sign at him. Mike let out a low sigh of relief, smiled, and nodded back. Everything had gone well on his front, too. Alibis established, they could hardly wait for the school day to be over. And like they'd done for the last few days, they huddled together out in the hall during PE and at lunch to discuss their secret adventure.

When the afternoon dismissal bell finally rang, Mike and Timbo didn't waste a second. They ran all the way home and straight up to Timbo's room. They had been gathering supplies all week and stashing them under Timbo's bed for safekeeping. Timbo pulled a checklist out of his pocket and started reading it aloud. "Two fishing poles?" Timbo asked.

"Check," Mike replied as he pulled them from under the bed.

"Two canteens, matches, and two flashlights?"

"Check, check, check," Mike confirmed.

"Two quilts and an old sheet?" Timbo asked as he folded up the list.

"Check, check again," Mike replied. "It's all here and ready to go. Now we just have to make a brief stop by the kitchen and grab some food for dinner."

"Well, what are we waiting for? Let's go," Timbo said.

Timbo and Mike grabbed the fishing gear, stuffed everything else into a duffel bag, and hurried toward the kitchen. There, they took a package of hot dogs, some cookies, a box of crackers, and some potato chips.

It didn't take long to throw everything into the canoe, and they were on their way. It was a beautiful afternoon, and Timbo and Mike made it to the island in no time flat. They floated around the back side so the boat would be hidden from view. Casually, Timbo tried to glance around the banks. Thankfully, he didn't see any alligators there.

Feeling Mike looking at him, Timbo explained, "Adventurers should always scope out new territory. And I was sure of it all along. There's not a single alligator within miles of here."

"Boy, that sure is a relief," Mike said as he hopped out of the front of the canoe and pulled it up on the muddy bank. "But, of course, I knew it all along, too."

It wasn't a big island. There was a small clump of trees that leaned down a bit toward the water on the back left side. Otherwise it consisted primarily of flat rocks piled up here and there and patches of grassy weeds blowing in the wind. It was everything and more than they had imagined. Running from one end to the other, Timbo and Mike fished for hours and collected handfuls of smooth stones as treasure. Whistling all the way and finally getting a little tired and hungry, they set up camp.

Timbo found four long sticks, pushed them into the soft dirt, and threw the old sheet across the top. Mike spread out the quilts underneath, and they both decided to sit for a while before making the campfire and roasting the hot dogs. Munching on their cracker appetizers, Timbo contentedly said, "Now, this is the life, isn't it?"

"Yep," Mike agreed. "It can't get any better than this."

And so, alone in the wilderness, underneath their makeshift tent, looking out at the full moon, they'd done it. Timbo and Mike were finally experiencing a real-life adventure.

But not for long. A big line of dark clouds started rolling in over the horizon, and before they could move, the stick tent was blown down by sheets of rain and heavy winds. It would pass over in a minute, they both thought, trying to make themselves feel better. But it didn't pass over. It rained harder and harder, and the wind blew stronger and stronger. Timbo and Mike were soaking wet under the sparse group of trees. That's when they heard a low, moaning, hissing sound through the wind. "Get off my island. Get off my island," it seemed to say.

"The ghost of Bleu. I always told you he was real," Mike whispered in fear as he turned to Timbo. Timbo had never seen Mike look so scared in his entire life.

"No, you didn't," Timbo whispered back. "I'm the one who always told you."

They both ran to the canoe. They had to get out of there. They had to go home.

When Timbo and Mike had almost made it to the safety of their drifting canoe, they stopped in their tracks. Something was moving by the canoe. Another bolt of lightning lit up the storm, and Timbo and Mike could see a huge alligator slithering up the banks toward them. It flashed a mouthful of pointy, scraggly teeth and made the most awful growling sound that they had ever heard.

"Oh, no," Mike moaned. "We're gonna die. The grown-ups were right. If old Bleu doesn't get us, then the alligator surely will. What do we do? What do we do?" Mike begged Timbo for an answer.

They both stood perfectly still. Maybe the alligator hadn't seen them yet. But he would, and then they would be eaten alive. Mike was frozen in fear, but thankfully Timbo wasn't.

"It's our only chance," Timbo said as he reached into the duffel bag and pulled out the only weapon they had. He threw their bag of food at the alligator. Snapping it up, the creature disappeared into the darkness to enjoy his dinner, giving Mike and Timbo just enough time to hop into the boat and paddle to safety.

The storm was subsiding now, and they knew they could make it across to Timbo's dock.

"Whoa, that was close. I've never been so scared in my entire life," Mike said, sighing.

But Timbo didn't answer. He was lost in his thoughts as his life flashed before his eyes. Strangely, he thought about his mother and her favorite picture of him. He was three years old and was wearing his favorite outfit—red cowboy boots, a red holster holding two little plastic pistols, and a red cowboy hat complete with white tassels hanging down over the brim—and was standing by his Shetland pony, Suzie. It was his mother's favorite photo, and she kept it in a tiny frame on her bedside table. He also thought about his sisters and how Santa Claus had needed some extra help last year, so he had stayed up all night, helping put together a wooden dollhouse, complete with all the furnishings. He was glad that he was okay. His family needed one another. They couldn't have done without him.

As the canoe slowly approached the dock, there was a crowd of neighbors waiting. Everybody had been going crazy looking for them. Evidently Timbo's mother had called over to Mike's house when the big storm was brewing. That's when word spread quickly that they were missing. Running out onto the dock, Timbo's mother cried tears of joy and wrapped them both in blankets to quiet their shivering. Timbo and Mike, somewhat in shock, could hear voices all around, saying, "It's a wonder they weren't eaten alive"; "It's a wonder they didn't drown."

But the nightmarish adventure was over. They were safe. Besides contracting terrible colds, they were going to live. And, of course, above all else, they were in big trouble. Timbo and Mike wouldn't be allowed even to go near the bayou for months to come.

Sitting in the Start Middle School classroom the following week, Timbo was just glad to be alive. Being grounded from the bayou hadn't been the worst thing in the world. And even though his mother still hadn't quite gotten over the scare, she wouldn't stay upset for too much longer. Timbo and Mike had decided to enter the short story contest after all, and they had just been announced as the winners for "The Ghost of Bayou Bleu." Of course it wasn't fiction, but they knew no one would really believe that. They hadn't.

★ ★ ★

In 1992, *Tim McGraw* exploded onto the country music scene. His debut single, "Indian Outlaw," was a smash hit and started him on a string of number one singles. The ballad "Don't Take the Girl" was a huge hit that helped push his album *Not a Moment Too Soon* to sales of more than five million—the fifth all-time best-selling album in any music category as of 1994.

Tim's 1996 Spontaneous Combustion tour brought his music to everybody, with sellout shows across the nation. It was listed as one of the top five tours of that year, and it changed his life. He and his touring mate, Faith Hill, married in Tim's hometown of Start, Louisiana, that same year. Ultimately, his 1997 album, *Everywhere,* produced five number one hits, and "Just to See You Smile" stayed on the *Billboard* record charts for forty-two weeks—longer than any other single in the modern history of the charts. His current album, *A Place in the Sun,* recently debuted at number one on both the country and pop album charts, and was named Album of the Year by the Country Music Association.

Tim was born in Louisiana and lived on the bayou. A talented baseball player, he says that he didn't pursue it as a career because he was too small. Rather, in college, he recalls playing his guitar for his friends and being a "closet singer." Memories from his life in Louisiana go back to the time when he was three and he would ride his Shetland pony, Suzie, all day on a well-worn path around the house in his favorite cowboy outfit. He will also never forget the Christmas that he helped Santa Claus put together a wooden dollhouse for his sisters. And, of course, there was the island. He and his friends used to go there and dig tunnels from one end to the other. There was one night, though, that they all got in trouble for carting the television, the radio, and all the food from the refrigerator out there for a cookout.

The Ugly Puppet

PATTY LOVELESS

My name is Petie, like Petie the dog on *The Little Rascals*—the one that has a big circle around one of his eyes. It's not my real name, of course, but my sister Dottie nicknamed me that when I was just a baby because of a temporary affliction that I had.

I had a disease in my eye called "shingles," and it made one whole side of my face look absolutely terrible. I was really sick and had to go to the hospital and stay for two whole weeks, and everybody visited me. It was awful, and the more we tell it the worse it gets. Now I think that I almost died.

The doctors say that my eye is completely cured and has been for years and years, but I don't believe it. Every day, I can see in the mirror that my left eye is more crooked and uglier than the other. Of course, my mother says it's purely my imagination and that I'm a pretty thing. I really believe her most of the time. But today, I know I'm not cured. I'm as ugly as this puppet, which is the very thing that I can't take to school today. That's what I've been telling Mother.

"Whatever happens, I just can't go to school," I kept saying over and over.

But she told me not to worry and that everything was going to be fine. When you're my age, there's not much use in arguing back. But this morning, just looking out the window up that hill makes me feel sick all over again. Trudging up there will be a long march to my certain death from humiliation.

We live in Pikeville, Kentucky, and at the very top of the hill beside our house is where I skip to catch the bus every day to go to the Elkhorn City School. And normally everything is just fine, like Mother says. Our little white frame house sort of sits in the curve at the bottom, and there's always smoke streaming out of the chimney. There's also a front porch

for sitting and talking or thinking of what to do next, and there's a big river running right behind us. It's the perfect place to play while Mother stays nonstop busy inside the house.

There's not much room to take care of where we live, but there's plenty of work to be done taking care of our big family. That's because I have six brothers and sisters. Even though three are already grown and have moved out on their own, that still leaves three more of us children and the baby. Everybody gets along just fine.

The baby stays in the room with Mother and Daddy, and I share a room with my brothers, which I actually don't mind a bit. I'm a tomboy in spirit and in fact. And since I don't have sisters at home anymore, I might as well be a boy. That is if you don't count my cousin Sue. She's fine, too, I guess.

She came to live with us for a while not long ago, but then she left and went back home again or off to some other relatives for a while, I'm not sure which. Mother says that country folks do visiting like that. They just kind of wander like one big family between relatives and stay and live for a while. Everybody thinks it's just fine. But one thing's for certain: Things aren't fine around here anymore.

If it wasn't for spelling, of all things, I wouldn't be in this mess. Normally, spelling's not a terrible thing. In fact, we have a spelling bee at school every Friday, and most of the time I can't wait. It's a fun game, and I'm pretty good at it. Usually I'm one of the ones left standing and spelling even if I don't end up winning the whole game. But yesterday my teacher thought it would be fun to add a new part to the spelling bee game. It sounded like a fine idea, but now I realize that it was one of those tricky homework assignments—the kind that sounds fun and ends up being awful.

The terrible project was to make a simple puppet to use to spell out our words during our next spelling bee. "Any old kind of puppet," the teacher suggested. She said the best kind would be simple and easy to make, maybe out of a paper bag, cutting out shapes for a face and decorating with crayons and a pencil. "Easy" was the key word she used, which sounded great to me at the time. I couldn't wait to step off the bus and run down the hill to gather my materials and make my puppet.

Racing through our front door, I searched around until I found exactly what I needed:

a small paper bag, some half-broken crayons that still worked fine, and some scissors. Mother wondered out loud what in the world I was doing, but I wouldn't tell my secret. I was going to unveil my wonderful piece of puppet artwork at supper.

At first, I drew a kind of plain dress like mine on the bag and decorated it with different crayon shapes and designs. So far, so good. Then I drew hair, and cut out two eyes, a nose, and a mouth. Overall it was pretty good, but I decided the eyes were too small. So, I carefully cut the right eye bigger, and that's when it happened. As I tried to make the left eye bigger, the scissors slipped, and bigger is definitely what I got. It was a lopsided, too-big eye that suddenly reminded me of my crooked left eye. In a matter of moments, it was an ugly puppet.

"Mama," I screamed, and she came running.

In a flurry of words and tears, I told her about the project and pointed to the ugly puppet on the floor—one huge eye stared at us, crumpled and uglier than ever. The crayon designs even looked ugly now, too.

"I just can't go to school tomorrow," I said over and over again.

Mother looked tired, but her eyes were sparkling like they always do. She reached down and gently picked up the ugly puppet and said, "Your puppet is fine. You'll be fine. It's going to be just fine."

"No, Mother," I said, "it won't be fine."

But Mother just repeated her gentle words until I went to bed and finally fell asleep.

Hearing my brothers, I woke up to the sun streaming through the window, looked out the window at the grassy hill, and thought for a long time. Mother always says that a good night's rest cures most things, but I knew that nothing could ever cure the ugly puppet—just like nothing can ever cure my eye, no matter what anybody says.

It's cold today, but the warm, sweet smell of cooking drifts around the corner, and for a moment I forget about the puppet and wonder what's for breakfast. There's never much variety, but it's always good. Maybe it's ham on rolls—or better yet, sweet rice. That's rice with butter and sugar and milk, and it's my favorite. Just the thought of such a treat is why I decide to get out of bed. I quickly grab my dress and a pair of pants to go under it to keep warm.

Running into the kitchen, I see that Mother has long finished baking, and my brothers are struggling into their clothes in front of the open stove door. That's where we all get dressed in the morning—around the stove—because it takes a while for the rest of the house to get warm. And today, there is sweet rice waiting. Perfect. Except for me and the ugly puppet.

Mother is trying to feed us and help us all get ready and out the door and up the hill to catch the bus. She tells my brothers to hurry up as they each grab a piece of corn bread for lunch and race out. But I lag behind, waiting for Mother to tell me to hurry up, too. That's when I'll tell her again that I'm not going to school today. But Mother doesn't say anything. She just motions me to the side and hands me something.

It's a puppet, and I suddenly realize Mother had stayed up most of the night as I slept and my ugly puppet lay crumpled on the floor. She had taken one of Dad's old black socks and sewed button eyes and a thin red mouth on it, and had also made a tiny dress out of scraps of pink material. It's the prettiest puppet that I have ever seen in my entire life. Not like a perfect, fancy, store-bought puppet—it was a different kind of pretty—but really pretty just the same. It was pretty because it was special. I guess a little like me.

"Thank you, Mother. Thank you so much," I say as I hug her as tight as I can.

I decide not to skip up the hill to catch the bus. I'm going to run. I can hardly wait to get to school. There's a lot to celebrate today. My puppet is not ugly, and I'm finally cured, too. Everything is just fine.

Patty Loveless was born Patty "Petie" Ramey and grew up in Pikeville, Kentucky. She was the sixth of seven children born to Naomi and John Ramey, who was a coal miner. Patty started singing when she was just five years old to entertain her father and mother, and by the time she was twelve she was singing in her brother Roger's band.

Patty signed her first record deal in 1985, and one of her first big hits was a song called "If My Heart Had Windows." In 1988 she was inducted into the Grand Ole Opry and has continued to have a long list of number one songs and albums ever since. Patty has been named Female Vocalist of the Year twice by the Academy of Country Music as well as earned a Female Vocalist of the Year award from the Country Music Association. In addition, she's made more than sixteen country music videos, ten of which have been number one hits on Country Music Television.

When she was little, Patty remembers watching her coal miner father return home all blackened with soot, and she talks often of the days she spent growing up in a small, white frame house. Patty's humble roots and love for country music are the reasons for her heartfelt, soulful sound—a sound that distinguishes her as Nashville's leading female traditionalist after more than a decade of recording.

A distant cousin of Loretta Lynn, Patty was a self-described tomboy. She grew up listening to country singers and musicians standing and playing on top of the custard stand at the Polly Anna Drive-in Theater and danced with her family every Saturday night, listening to the Grand Ole Opry radio show. It is true that she did suffer from shingles when she was just four years old, and the house and the river were just as she described. The ugly puppet was an actual incident—one that Patty remembers poignantly.

Listen to the Mockingbird

VINCE GILL

Way up north of a little town in Oklahoma called Edmond, the pool hall was all lit up with activity. It was tournament night, and it was standing room only. The jukebox was blaring, but no one seemed to notice. Even with the bright neon wall lights that seemed to flash with the beat of whatever was playing, it was still dark around the edges and hard to make out all the faces. But one thing was certain: All eyes were on the player—everyone was watching and waiting and holding their breath. His final shot for the win was going to be almost impossible to make.

The player's name was Grant. He had been back and forth to the pool hall many times to play with his fifth-grade buddies, but until lately he had never, ever won. It had seemed obvious that Grant hadn't inherited his family's talent for the game.

Everybody in Grant's family played pool—his dad, his granddad, and probably back further. And they were all really good. In fact, there had been a snooker table in Grant's family for as long as he could remember. Not pool, mind you, but snooker. And if you've ever seen a snooker table or played on one, you'll appreciate the difference right away. It's a much more difficult game than pool. The pockets are smaller, and the balls are smaller, which all adds up to harder. So if you could even halfway play snooker, you sure enough would never have a problem playing on a big pool table. "It's kind of like stealing," Grant's dad would say.

More than anything Grant wanted to be a good pool player, too, and he would rush home every day after school to practice on the snooker table. But even though he tried and tried, Grant just wasn't able to play the game very well. He didn't believe that he'd ever be able to do it. Then, something extraordinary happened on a weekend family outing. His wish finally came true in the form of a pet bird.

Often, Grant and his family would travel not far from their town to a place called Stover Hall, in Piedmont, Oklahoma. It was an open-air music hall, and the bluegrass players there were some of the best around. Everyone in Grant's family loved to go hear the music, and one of their favorite musicians was the star bluegrass performer Herman Stover. Without fail, he'd play "Listen to the Mockingbird," where he'd make bird sounds with his fiddle—bird sounds that were so real, you could hardly believe they weren't. And Grant had never believed it. There had to be a mockingbird inside that fiddle or somewhere near, and he was going to find it.

The very next time the family went to Stover Hall, Grant sat there and listened through the first few songs. When Herman Stover announced that he was going to play "Listen to the Mockingbird" next, Grant eased away and crept behind the wooden platform stage.

Sure enough, there was a real-life mockingbird sitting free on a small wooden ledge, getting ready to sing its heart out on cue. "I knew it," he whispered in triumph about the same time that the mockingbird made a light, graceful jump off its resting place and landed on Grant's shoulder.

Lost in the unexpected moment, Grant never heard whether Herman Stover had tried to play "Listen to the Mockingbird" without the bird helping, and so he never heard him coming, either. But all of a sudden, Herman Stover was standing right there, staring at Grant. *Uh-oh,* Grant thought. *I'm in big trouble now.*

Trying to explain himself, Grant started gesturing wildly in an attempt to get the bird off his shoulder, and words started tumbling out of his mouth almost faster than anyone could understand them. "Excuse me, Mr. Stover," Grant began quickly. " I wasn't trying to bother your bird. It just came by itself and sat on my shoulder, and I wasn't going to take it or anything. I was just going to see . . . well, my name is Grant and we come here all the time, and I just knew that you kept a mockingbird inside your fiddle. I just wanted to see it for myself."

Mr. Stover stood there a minute, looking back and forth from the bird to Grant—most likely trying to think of the worst punishment imaginable, the boy thought. From the dusty ground up, Stover had on a pair of shiny, pointy black boots, and then an ivory-colored suit with big pockets on the jacket that parted to show a thin black ribbon with silver tips on the end, which was tied in a floppy bow under his stiff, starched collar. Finally you came to a wise, gentle face with eyes that were dancing with laughter and one of the kindest smiles ever

that spread out to meet his wrinkly cheeks. He wasn't mad at all; in fact, he looked happy.

Herman Stover knelt down. Chuckling, he explained, "That bird can't sing a lick. In fact, he really doesn't do much of anything but sit and keep me company. He came here years ago, and I've kept him as a pet ever since. I finally named him Lucky because he's stayed with me through thick and thin. But now it looks like he's found a new friend. You must be the very one who needs him now." Not allowing a split second for Grant to disagree, Mr. Stover continued. "Take him and go, young man. You just never know when you'll need a little luck. Believe me."

And with the bird still sitting on Grant's shoulder, Mr. Stover handed him the tiny wooden perch, tipped his hat, and disappeared behind the stage curtain. Whether he liked it or not, Grant was the proud new owner of Lucky the pet bird.

Just about everywhere he went from then on, Grant's pet bird Lucky went, too—riding shotgun on his shoulder. And remembering what Mr. Stover had said, Grant wasn't at all surprised that he started playing pool so much better. Practicing at home unnoticed, he kept getting better and better, and all the time, Lucky was there. Grant knew that Lucky was a good luck charm, and he finally decided to show everybody else by challenging one of the best players at the pool hall one evening.

Everybody in the pool hall roared with laughter. "We wouldn't feel right about taking money from a baby! Or is his bird going to play for him?"

"Leave my bird alone," said Grant.

It was an odd moment. Grant was standing there with a bird sitting on his shoulder, and he was armed with a stick in his hand that was almost taller than he was. But when someone finally agreed to play with him, that was the beginning of the end. Grant won game after game that evening from a waiting room of seasoned players.

"Beginner's luck," everyone grumbled as Grant and Lucky finally called it quits.

After a few more visits like that one, it was obvious that it wasn't beginner's luck. Grant was really, really good. With the bird perched on his shoulder, he had beaten everybody around, and now he was a finalist in the city tournament.

It was the perfect story, and word started to spread quickly. There were even pictures of Grant and Lucky on the main television station and in the local newspapers, all telling the story and promoting tournament day.

YOUNG BOY AND PET BIRD LUCKY FAVORED TO WIN THE CITY TOURNAMENT, one headline read.

BOY SAYS LUCKY BIRD WILL BOOST HIM TO VICTORY AGAIN, said another.

As a result, tournament tickets had been sold out for weeks, with people coming from miles around to see the famous boy and his pet bird. Herman Stover had even sent a note saying that he wouldn't miss it for the world.

The morning of the tournament—the biggest day of his life—Grant woke up with a start. Something was the matter, but he didn't know what. He flung himself out of bed, threw on his clothes that were still lying on the floor from the night before, and grabbed his baseball hat. "Lucky." He whistled. "Get up and come on. It's our big day."

And that's when he noticed: Lucky wasn't sitting on his wooden perch by the window. "Come on, Lucky, quit hiding. I want to go practice some. This will be one of our toughest games, and everybody's going to be there watching." But Lucky was nowhere to be found.

Grant ran down the stairs, hollering for Lucky the whole way. He looked in the cabinets, under the steps, through the laundry, and there still wasn't a sign of Lucky anywhere.

"He's somewhere, Grant. You'll find him in time. Just calm down," his mother said.

But Grant wouldn't hear of it. He went out the front door shouting, and before long there was a search party of neighbors and townspeople looking for the bird. Word spread fast that Grant's bird Lucky was missing, and everyone started thinking about the tournament that night.

What would Grant do without Lucky? How would he play? Surely, someone would find the bird by then. But the whole day sped by and turned into evening. It was time for the tournament. "Believe me, Grant. You're a fine pool player with or without Lucky," Grant's dad reassured him.

There was a crowd waiting outside the pool hall, and reporters were gathered all around, speculating whether the boy wonder could be expected to win the tournament without his good luck bird. Grant marched slowly and silently through the crowd and went inside to get it over with. He felt sure it wouldn't be a long game.

But the next hour went by in a flash, with Grant still hanging in there without Lucky. Unlike most of his games, though, he was missing shots he normally could have made with his eyes closed. And he was behind a lot of the time. It had been grueling, but now it was almost over.

People were standing on chairs and peeking through the windows to get a good look. It was Grant's last shot, an almost impossible one. He didn't believe he could do it. There was too much pressure, and Lucky wasn't there to help him. It was over. Grant froze.

Breaking the hushed silence, people started chanting, "Come on, Grant. You can do it. You can do it." Over and over they kept saying it.

And then suddenly, blended in at first with the sea of voices, a fiddle started playing—slow and quiet at first, the familiar tune gradually overtook the room. It was "Listen to the Mockingbird," and everybody turned around to see Herman Stover playing in the doorway.

Grant dropped his stick, and with everyone wondering what in the world was going on, he walked over to Herman Stover to get Lucky out of the fiddle. But Lucky wasn't there, and Grant didn't believe it.

"I need to have Lucky back, Mr. Stover," Grant said. "I can't win without him."

"Why, sure you can. Just like I can play the fiddle without him. That's why I'm sure that Lucky has gone to find someone who needs him, because it is indeed lucky to have something to believe in—just for a while, just to get you started. Go on, young man. Believe me," Herman Stover urged as he tipped his hat and disappeared through the doorway.

Grant walked back to the table. You could have heard a pin drop. Everybody was watching and waiting. In order to win, Grant would have to make an almost impossible shot. It would be very difficult, especially without the bird.

Grant picked up the pool cue, surveyed the pool table, and suddenly realized that he knew exactly how to make the shot. That's when he quietly said, "Okay, I will believe. I do believe. This once, I do believe." And with that, he made his last shot for the right corner pocket.

The ball crept down the table. Slowly, slowly, it wasn't going to make it. Slowly, slowly, it was rolling to a stop less than half an inch from the pocket. No one moved. It appeared as if the ball was definitely going to stop. And it did. The ball finally stopped when it dropped into the pocket.

He'd done it, and the crowd went wild. Grant had won the city tournament all by himself. And he deserved it. He was a good pool player. His practice had paid off. He just needed somebody to believe in him. Not Mr. Stover. Not Lucky. Not his dad. Not the cheering crowd. Grant only needed to believe in himself. And as several of the happy fans picked him up and lifted him high in the air, Grant felt proud. Grant felt lucky.

* * *

Vince Grant Gill grew up in Oklahoma as the son of a banjo-playing federal judge. Showing his musical prowess early, Vince joined a high school bluegrass band, Mountain Smoke, which gained enough popularity to open a concert for the pop group Pure Prairie League. After high school, though, Vince considered a career as a professional golfer until he was invited to join a Louisville bluegrass band called the Bluegrass Alliance. After a year with them, he moved to Los Angeles to play with a band there and, coincidentally enough, was offered a job with Pure Prairie League. Vince sang the lead vocals on three of their albums and on the pop hit "Let Me Love You Tonight."

Landing his first solo recording contract in 1983, Vince recorded three RCA albums that yielded several top ten hits. But his first MCA album, recorded in 1989 and entitled *When I Call Your Name,* established him as a superstar in country music. The title song won a GRAMMY Award, and the album eventually sold one million copies. Since then, every one of Vince's six MCA albums has sold a million copies or more, and his numerous awards now include ten GRAMMYs and seventeen awards from the Country Music Association.

Growing up in Oklahoma, Vince came from a long line of pool players. Everybody in his family played pool, and everybody played well. Even in grade school, Vince enjoyed visiting and playing pool with his brother, who was enrolled in a nearby college. In fact, he laughs when he says that there was a saying in Oklahoma that if you were a good pool player, then you must have "led a misspent youth." He also liked to go with his family on the weekends to Stover Hall, where their favorite performer was Herman Stover. Hearing "Listen to the Mockingbird," Vince remembers actually believing that there was a mockingbird inside the fiddle.

The Coat of Many Colors

DOLLY PARTON

This is the story of a girl. A very different girl, unlike anyone around. She had yellow hair, the fairest of skin, the most extraordinary blue-green eyes, and the voice of an angel. A princess, she lived in one of the prettiest valleys between some of the very oldest mountains in the entire world. There, among the meandering streams and velvet moss–covered forests, she was wealthy beyond measure. Audiences of thousands of people would gather round to listen to her sing the most wonderful stories.

"Rebecca, Rebecca," the teacher said.

Mr. Parker had gone through the entire school to collect the required book reports from each and every student. It hadn't taken him long: The Mountainview schoolhouse had only one room, with a total of twenty-five students all bunched together in grades one through seven. Lost back in the mountains far away from the rest of the world, the tiny schoolhouse served many children who were from very poor families. Some of those students had to walk up a winding dirt road for over two and a half miles each morning before they finally got there. In the gusty, snowy mountain winters, the poor children would arrive like little, lost, frozen urchins and have to thaw out in front of the schoolhouse woodstove before they could begin their lessons.

Mr. Parker knew each and every one of them like sons and daughters, and Rebecca was one of his favorites, despite her tendency to daydream. She got away with it, though, because somehow Rebecca had been blessed with the best memory the teacher had ever seen. No matter what Mr. Parker assigned, Rebecca would learn it very quickly and could recite it back in no time at all with hardly a mistake. Therefore, she didn't have to work very hard on her lessons like all the other struggling students. That gave Rebecca plenty of time to pretend, and here she was once again looking out the window and letting her vivid imagination run wild.

"Rebecca," Mr. Parker said one last time.

Rebecca glanced up and realized that she was no longer a princess sitting in the meadow singing for thousands. "Yes, sir," she replied.

"We are all waiting for you to read your book report." The teacher tried to sound stern, despite his fondness.

Everybody knew that Rebecca wouldn't read from her written report. She never did. Rebecca was a born storyteller, and whether she had memorized her report or not, she preferred to stand alone in front of the class and let her imagination run wild. With patches on her coveralls and holes in both her shoes, she would rise from her school-desk throne, skip up to her classroom stage, and end up telling the longest, most involved stories you've ever heard. And, no matter what it was about, she'd inevitably end it by talking about the day when she was going to be a princess. Wrapped up in her own drama time and time again, Rebecca would finally realize that all the children were laughing at her.

"Quit trying to show off, Rebecca," they scolded. "You're not going to be a princess. You're just making things up like you always do."

Maintaining her composure, Rebecca would always say, "It doesn't matter what you think," as she would go back to her throne with the teacher smiling the whole way.

★ ★ ★

Mr. Parker knew that there weren't many people in those mountains who were as creative and as hopeful as Rebecca, particularly when there was so little chance of things changing. As it had always been, generation after generation was destined to pass down a burdensome inheritance of obscurity and poverty. Almost certainly, it wouldn't be any different for Rebecca.

However, Rebecca hadn't yet realized her hopeless circumstances. She believed in her dreams, and as always, she would seemingly forget the endless teasing and taunting. The long walk home from school had proved to be the best medicine for healing hurtful words. Lost in her imagination, she'd sing all the way like a little wounded bird until she got home, where she would be able to fly free again.

When she was almost to the end of her journey each day, Rebecca would gasp with delight at the sight of her enormous castle set among the tall, leafy trees and forever blossoming flowers. Her father was the king who spent most of his time away surveying his land. With blond hair just like hers, he was a kind, wise king who was able to command the most beautiful vegetables right out of the ground for everyone to eat. And he had placed a wishing well right outside that housed an endless supply of the most sought-after crystal-clear mountain water.

Once inside, Rebecca would tiptoe across the wide wooden floors made of the finest oak and would glance at the beautiful tapestries that adorned the walls. And then, she'd feel the indescribable warmth that radiated from her mother's presence. An Indian princess long ago, her mother was like a beautiful picture, with dark, shiny hair cascading down upon her shoulders. She would sing stories while sewing the most lovely garments and linens in the entire kingdom. To Rebecca, everything was beyond compare. She was a princess. But, of course, that was from the inside looking out, not the outside looking in.

"Rebecca, Rebecca," her father called.

Suddenly, Rebecca wasn't a princess living in a peaceful valley. She was an everyday Cinderella who lived down in a holler in a small, weathered shack at the end of a bumpy dirt road. Far from a castle on the inside, you could see the chickens running around under the house through the cracks in the old, creaky plank floors. And the wall coverings were nothing more than old, yellowed newspapers pasted here and there so the wind couldn't blow snow inside. There was no indoor plumbing and no running water, which accounted for the rusty old well outside. Plus, it was crowded. There were twelve children being raised up behind those meager walls, and that meant having to sleep with four or five to a small bed.

Making things better under such hard circumstances was a constant struggle, even though Rebecca's father, Lee, worked hard to provide for his family. They had moved often, from one shack to another, so he could look for patches of land that would grow vegetables and tobacco to sell. And sometimes he'd have to travel for a while just to find work.

Rebecca's mother, Avie Lee, did the very best she could, too. Taking care of twelve children kept her busy enough. They wouldn't have had much of anything unless she made it. There was hardly ever any money for store-bought things. So from making soap and grinding meal to fashioning corncob dolls and sewing patchwork quilts, it was all homemade. They were without a doubt one of the poorest families around, having nothing of any material value.

But with strength and an abundance of love, the family always seemed to make ends meet. No questions asked, everybody pitched in. Except for Rebecca.

"Rebecca, Rebecca," her father called again and again. "Where is that child?" he mumbled. *Most likely out imagining something or the other,* he thought. *What am I going to do with her?*

When all the others would help gather potatoes, Rebecca would fall in line, singing, leaving the potatoes and picking up odd-shaped stones instead. "You're falling behind, Rebecca," her father would yell from the front of the plow. "Drop all that junk now and help out."

"Oh, no, Daddy," Rebecca chirped. "They're my jewels for the day that I'm going to be a princess."

Because of the family's heavy workload, Rebecca didn't get much sympathy. If anything, her brothers and sisters were always mad and jealous that she never ended up doing her share of the chores. It was perplexing to a father like Lee, who had never known anything but hard work, and he blamed it all on her mother. While Avie Lee would quilt every evening, she'd tell story after story, with Rebecca sitting at her feet.

"You're putting all this nonsense in her head, Avie Lee," Rebecca's father would say. But he could have talked until he was blue in the face. It wouldn't have mattered. Even with eleven others to mind, Avie Lee had always felt a certain kinship with Rebecca. She understood the need to have hopes and dreams, even if her own hadn't come true. And thinking on these things late one night, Avie Lee made a decision.

It was going to be winter soon, and each child still fit into a used, worn coat—all except Rebecca. So, Avie Lee decided to make her a special coat—a special coat for her favorite child. And she had just enough of the multicolored scraps left that well-meaning neighbors would drop on her doorstep for quilting. As Avie Lee began sewing stitch by stitch, she told Rebecca the most wonderful story.

It was the story of a handsome boy named Joe. He had lots of brothers, but he was the youngest, and he got most all of the attention. His dad loved him the best and brought him home a very expensive and special gift one day. It was a coat, hand sewn with the finest materials and woven in the most beautiful array of colors. In his coat, Joe pranced around and told his brothers that he was going to be a king one day. And in their laughter, they were jealous of Joe and mocked him for saying that he was to be king. But as the story ended, Joe did in fact go on to become a king.

Hearing her mother tell the story again and again while sewing each square, Rebecca couldn't wait for her coat of many colors to be finished. It was going to be the most beautiful coat ever, and her mother was making it just for her. Even before her mother finished, Rebecca would beg and beg to put it on just for a second. Then she'd dance around the tiny room while each and every one of her brothers and sisters watched with jealousy. They would especially get mad when she said, "See, I told you that I was going to be a princess someday. This fine coat proves it."

Finally one night the coat was finished, and Rebecca proudly wore it all around. It didn't appear as if she was going to ever take it off. But since everybody was sick of hearing how beautiful it was and it was bedtime, Avie Lee took it for safekeeping until the next day.

"Even though it's not cold outside yet, you can wear it tomorrow to school if you'd like. Now go on to sleep," her mother said as she lovingly blessed the coat with a kiss.

That night, Rebecca hardly slept, just waiting to wear her coat to school. She knew all the other children would be as jealous as her brothers and sisters. Even when it did get cold, none of them would be wearing a new coat. And so now, they couldn't possibly help but realize how special Rebecca was. There wouldn't be a doubt in anyone's mind that she was going to be a princess someday. She felt certain.

Rebecca made a grand entrance into the schoolhouse the next morning and proudly stood—waiting for everyone to admire her and her new coat. And standing there, it wasn't hard for Rebecca to imagine that she was, in fact, a princess. That is until she looked up and realized that all the students were laughing and pointing at her.

"Don't you see my new coat?" Rebecca said to one of the boys.

"I don't see any new coat. I just see a bunch of funny-colored rags," he sneered.

Rebecca thought she must be hearing wrong. Surely everyone could see how beautiful and special the coat was—how special *she* was. But turning to the other students, Rebecca saw that they were teasing her, too.

"You must be mighty poor to have to wear old scraps," they said.

"If I was you, I'd take that ugly thing off and throw it in the fire."

On and on, the students wouldn't stop laughing and making fun of her and telling her to take it off. Rebecca's heart was finally broken, but she raised her head high and kept her coat on. She ignored their teasing hour after hour until, mercifully, the school day was finally over. And on her long walk home, lost in her thoughts, Rebecca decided she'd never take the coat off. She'd wear it proudly all the way until she was a princess.

★ ★ ★

And so, there once was a woman. A very, very different woman, unlike anyone around. She had yellow hair, the fairest of skin, and the most extraordinary blue-green eyes. She lived in one of the prettiest valleys between some of the very oldest mountains in the world. And there, among the meandering streams and velvet moss–covered forests, she was wealthy beyond measure. Audiences of thousands of people would gather round as she sang this wonderful song:

Back through the years, I go wandering once again
Back to the seasons of my youth.
I recall a box of rags that someone gave us.
And how my Mama put the rags to use.

There were rags of many colors, but ev're piece was small.
And I didn't have a coat and it was way down in the Fall.
Mama sewed the rags together, sewing every piece with love,
She made my coat of many colors that I was so proud of.

As she sewed she told a story from the Bible she had read,
About a coat of many colors Joseph wore and then she said,
Perhaps this coat will bring you good luck and happiness,
And I just couldn't wait to wear it.
And Mama blessed it with a kiss.

My coat of many colors that my Mama made for me.
Made only from rags, but I wore it so proudly.
Although we had no money, I was rich as I could be
In my coat of many colors that my Mama made for me.

So with patches on my britches and holes in both my shoes,
In my coat of many colors, well I hurried off to school,
Just to find the others laughing and making fun of me
In my coat of many colors my Mama made for me.

And, oh, I couldn't understand it for I felt I was rich,
And I told them of the love my Mama sewed in every stitch,
And I told them all the story Mama told me while she sewed,
And how my coat of many colors was worth more
Than all their clothes.

But they didn't understand it and I tried to make them see
That one is only poor only if they choose to be.
Now I know we had no money, but I was rich as I could be
In my coat of many colors my Mama made for me.

✦ ✦ ✦

Dolly Parton is an internationally renowned superstar whose career spans four decades. In addition to "Coat of Many Colors," she's written and made famous such songs as "Jolene," "Here You Come Again," and "I Will Always Love You." Dolly has also starred in the Oscar-nominated film *9 to 5,* with Jane Fonda and Lily Tomlin, as well as *Rhinestone,* with Sylvester Stallone, and *Steel Magnolias,* with Julia Roberts, Sally Field, and Shirley MacLaine, to name a few. In 1986 she opened Dollywood, an entertainment theme park located in Pigeon Forge, Tennessee, designed to preserve her Smoky Mountain heritage and east Tennessee lifestyle.

Dolly Rebecca Parton was born in Sevier County, Tennessee, the fourth of twelve children born to Robert Lee and Avie Lee Parton. When she was just nine years old, Dolly appeared on the Sevierville radio station, WSEV, and by the age of ten she was performing professionally on both television and radio in nearby Knoxville, Tennessee.

With the dream of being a country music singer, Dolly moved to Nashville the day after she graduated from high school, and by the time she was twenty-one, Porter Wagoner hired her to join the cast of his popular television show. From there, she quickly climbed the ladder of success. A four-time GRAMMY Award winner and an Oscar nominee, Dolly Parton is a superstar performer, songwriter, actress, recording artist, and humanitarian.

This story is based on a true experience that inspired Parton to write the song "Coat of Many Colors." She has said that it is still her favorite song she has ever written or sung. Not to mention that it was also a very big hit.

Keep Out!

LORETTA LYNN

"Loretty, whatcha doin' puttin' up that sign? Ain't you caused enough trouble today?" her father hollered down the ridge.

Thirteen-year-old Loretta Webb was standing on her barefooted tiptoes. She was holding an old, half-rotten piece of wood with the words KEEP OUT crudely etched on it.

"Strangers ain't comin' here no more, Daddy," Loretta yelled back up.

"Nobody's comin' to bother you, Loretty," her daddy said, chuckling as he waved down to her and turned to go back inside their tiny four-room cabin in the Holler—a clearing in the mountains.

"Just the same, I've decided I ain't gonna give 'em another chance," Loretta replied stubbornly. She picked up the hammer she'd brought from her daddy's toolshed, reached into her pocket, and grabbed the rusty nail she'd found under the porch. Then she pounded the sign high onto a leaning fence post.

"There, now. That'll do it." Loretta smiled as she wiped her hands down the front of her shirt and climbed back up the ridge toward home. She was headed toward their sagging front porch to feed Donald Ray.

Every afternoon, Loretta helped her mother with the baby. There were seven Webb children so far, including her; she was the second oldest, and the newest member of the clan was baby Donald. He hadn't weighed very much when he was born, and therefore he needed lots of special attention to grow strong. But Loretta didn't mind. One of her favorite times of the day was rocking baby Donald on the front porch, all the while singing to him or telling him stories.

As Loretta sat down in the rocking chair on the porch with the baby cradled in her

arms, she said, "Daddy don't rightly understand 'bout strangers, but I'm gonna tell you all 'bout it, baby." So as she began to rock the tiny infant, Loretta started telling her story.

"You gotta understand. We Holler people mostly stay to ourselves. We don't know much of what goes on down below, and the city folks don't know much of what goes on up here. Mommy says it's better that way. 'We got everything we need right here,' she always says.

"It's a good thing that we do, 'cause gettin' back and forth to the Holler is mighty hard. My little schoolhouse is only 'bout halfway up the mountain, and from there you gotta walk another two miles up a curvy dirt road before you get to our place. Along the way, there's a pretty creek runnin' beside the path, but as you keep walkin' up the Holler, it gets steeper and steeper, and there are big ol' trees that just wrap you up on both sides. I know the way good, but it's a far piece from almost anywhere. So I reckon that's why there ain't many people that come callin' to the Holler.

"Now, I ain't talkin' 'bout company. Company's folks you know—like the mountain folk who come to fetch some of Mommy's plant medicine when they're sick, or some of our own kinfolk. I ain't talkin' 'bout them. I'm talkin' 'bout strangers—people who ain't from round here. People you ain't ever seen before in your entire life. Those kinda folks are different. They sometimes bring good news, but when it's all said and done, the bad outweighs the good. 'Least that's how I see it.

"You listenin', baby?" Loretta looked down at Donald Ray cradled in her arms. When her familiar voice stopped, he looked up and started to whimper. Seeing that he was far from going to sleep, Loretta continued.

"The first time a stranger came callin' was when I was little. I was only 'bout seven years old. Me and cousin Marie were playin' in the yard, and then, almost out of nowhere, a man walked up. He was all official-like, wearin' fancy clothes and holdin' a little suitcase. Well, 'course we run and hid round behind the side of the house.

"Mommy's always sayin', 'You younguns act like little wild rabbits.' But that ain't so. All of us Holler kids are bashful, and we ain't gonna talk to anybody until we know rightly who they are and what they want. And even then, I usually act kinda dumblike. Our uncle

Lee taught us to do that early on. He lives farther up the ridge from us, and the law is always tryin' to catch him makin' his moonshine. So he's always tellin' us that Holler people don't tell their goings-on . . . ever.

"So, anyway, I heard this stranger talkin' to Daddy. 'Howdy, Mr. Webb,' he said. 'I'm Jim Barnes, from the WPA. We've got a check here for you and some clothes for the children.'

"Now, when I heard that he had somethin' for me, I came creepin' out from behind the porch.

"'Well, well,' the man said when he saw me. 'I was wondering when you were going to come out. You sure are a pretty little thing.'

"The man put the suitcase flat on the ground and opened it up. And you won't hardly believe what was inside for me. It was a real store-boughten dress. The first one I'd ever had. It was blue with pink flowers, and little pockets on each side. It was plum beautiful.

"'Where's your manners, Loretty? Ain't ya gonna tell Mr. Barnes thank ya?' Daddy said.

"'Thank ya, sir,' I said as I took the dress and hugged it tight. Oh, how I loved that dress. And I got to thinkin' then. That stranger wasn't so bad after all. In fact, after he had given out some more clothes to Mommy, we were all smilin' and thankin' him. Daddy said that Mr. Barnes was a fine man and that he worked for a company that gave jobs and money to the coal miners when times was hard. I thought that was right nice, too, as I hurried to put on my new dress."

★　★　★

"After I put it on, Daddy kept sayin', 'Now don't get your new dress dirty, Loretty.' But he didn't need to tell me that. I was real careful to take good care of my pretty new store-boughten dress. That is until I'd worn it so much that I finally had to put it in the clothes pile on the porch for Mommy to wash. That's the last time I saw that dress. The hog was runnin' loose that day, and he just snatched my dress right off the porch and chewed it all to pieces. I hadn't got another store-boughten one since.

"Mommy said, 'You shoulda been more careful, Loretty.' Oh, I knew I should have, and I cried and cried. I wished that stranger had never come and give me anything. Better not to have it in the first place. Yep, baby. The good visit from that ol' stranger turned out real bad."

Loretta kept rocking back and forth as she continued talking to baby Donald. The singsong rhythm of her voice was soothing to the infant, and he appeared as if he understood every single word she was saying. Lost in her story, Loretta continued.

"So, the next time a stranger came up to the Holler, I was even more suspicious than ever. I hoped he hadn't brought somethin' good that would turn out bad. But this time, it was the 'xact opposite. The bad happened first.

"It was a couple of years ago that Daddy hadn't been feelin' good for a long time. He had breathed too much coal dust, and Mommy had been doctorin' him the best she could. Whenever there's anything wrong up on our Holler, Mommy will take care of it. But this time, Daddy wasn't gettin' any better, even with Mommy's help. That's when the next stranger came up here way in the middle of the night. I didn't know then where he came from—now I know it was the big hospital miles and miles away—but he appeared just the same, banged on the door, woke us all up, and Mommy went runnin' to help get Daddy.

"Mommy turned to me and said, 'Loretty, hurry and fetch a blanket.'

"I went and got my favorite quilt that Mommy had made out of Daddy's old overalls and carried it to her. She gently wrapped it around Daddy and helped the man carry him out the door. All of us kids were cryin' 'cause we didn't know why that man was takin' Daddy away and why Mommy was lettin' him.

"I hollered to Mommy, 'Where's Daddy goin'? When's he comin' back? Don't let that man take Daddy.'

"Then, somebody said, 'Your daddy won't be back.' I coulda swore that ol' stranger was the one who had said it as he took Daddy down the Holler on an old wooden sled.

"Mommy grabbed me tight to keep me from followin' Daddy, and she said, 'Hush up, Loretty. It's for the best. He's gonna try to help Daddy. I've done all I can.'

"I was sure the strange man wasn't goin' to try to help Daddy. He was takin' Daddy away and never bringin' him back. He said so. I cried and cried again—harder than I ever cried over that store-boughten dress. Day after day, I screamed down the Holler, 'Come back, Daddy. Please come back.' Mommy said that I must have screamed so loud that Daddy heard me all the way down at that hospital, because it wasn't long before he came home.

"I was glad that stranger hadn't brought Daddy back—Uncle Willie did—but Mommy said that I ought to be ashamed. She said that if it hadn't been for that man, Daddy would have died. Maybe so, but it took me a long time to quit thinkin' 'bout that man. I hoped I'd never see him ever again.

"See what I mean 'bout them strangers, baby?" Loretta said as she rocked back and forth and gazed down at her tiny little brother.

Baby Donald was quiet but still wide awake in Loretta's arms.

"You gotta go to sleep, baby, so you'll grow big and strong," Loretta urged. "If I tell you one last story, will you go to sleep?"

Baby Donald looked up at Loretta and smiled.

"Okay," Loretta said, "just one more."

Loretta pulled baby Donald closer to her as she rocked and continued her story.

"I'll finish tellin' you 'bout the very last time a stranger came callin'. This time, we knew he was comin'. Daddy told us.

"It was just yesterday when Daddy came home and said, 'I've got a big surprise for you younguns. Mr. Lewis is comin' tomorrow to bring you somethin' special.'

"So I asked, 'Do ya know Mr. Lewis, Daddy?'

"And Daddy said, 'Why, sure I do.'

"I thought about the other times that strangers had come, and I said, 'Well, I don't know him, and I don't want him comin' here.'

"Mommy laughed, and Daddy said, 'Don't act a fool, Loretty.'

"Daddy's word was always final, so it didn't matter in the end what I said or what I thought. This very afternoon, that strange man named Mr. John Lewis came callin' on us. Mommy said he was the boss of Daddy's coal union. I didn't know what that 'xactly meant. All I knew was that he was supposed to be important, and I was supposed to be nice. I told Mommy that I would be nice as long as the man didn't do somethin' bad like all the other strangers had.

"Mommy just shook her head and said, 'Now, don't be actin' silly, Loretty.'

"I tried not to act silly like Mommy said, but when Mr. Lewis came right after dinnertime, I was scared half to death. First off, he was a really big man—even taller than Daddy.

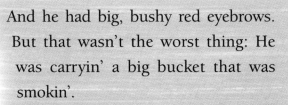

And he had big, bushy red eyebrows. But that wasn't the worst thing: He was carryin' a big bucket that was smokin'.

"Daddy called all us children and said, 'Hurry on up, everybody. Mr. Lewis has brought us some real vanilla ice cream.'

"None of us—not even Mommy or Daddy—had ever had real ice cream. The only kind we'd ever had was the Holler kind that Mommy made: ice cream made right out of the mountain snow, with milk and sugar on it. So we were all really excited to taste it. But me and brother Junior were curious first off about that smoke.

"You see, caked round the outside of that big ol' bucket was somethin' hard and white like ice, but it couldn't have been ice, because it was smokin'. And I knew it sure couldn't have been ice cream. That's when Mr. Lewis took the lid off the bucket, and sure enough I could see creamy ice cream on the inside. It sure looked good, but I still couldn't figure out what the icy stuff was that was smokin' on the outside. Junior was wonderin' about it, too.

"Everybody was gathered round

the bucket, and Mr. Lewis was dishin' out helpin's for everybody. Me and Junior kinda stood to the side, and I whispered to him, 'What do you think it is?'

"I meant for him to ask, but Junior decided that he wasn't goin' to ask. He was just goin' to find out for himself. So, while everybody was walkin' to the porch with their helpin' of ice cream, Junior went over to the bucket, reached down, and grabbed a piece of the smokin' ice to see for himself what it was. And as quick as you please, Junior dropped it on the ground and yelled, 'Ouch!'

"Mr. Lewis turned round on the porch and hollered, 'You better leave that alone, boy. You'll get burned.'

"Me and Junior didn't understand what he was talkin' 'bout, and we both started laughin'. Who'd ever heard of ice cream burnin' ya?

"'I knew it,' I said to Junior. 'He's just tryin' to trick us. See, I'll show ya.'

"And before all the ice-cream eaters on the porch could stop me, I reached down and grabbed a piece of the smokin' ice real tight.

"'Oooww!' I screamed so loud that Uncle Lee came down a little while later and told Daddy that he had heard me way up on the ridge.

"The smokin' ice was stuck to my fingers, and it was burnin' somethin' awful. I shook and shook my hand until the hot ice finally fell to the ground and part of me went with it. The skin of my very fingertips was almost burnt right off.

"'That'll teach ya,' Daddy said as he hurried over to me and looked at my hand. 'But I think you'll live,' he said. 'Now come on over here. Your ice cream's 'bout melted.'

"I didn't want any of that stranger's hot ice cream. I didn't care if I ever had that kinda ice cream again. And for sure, I knew that Mommy and Daddy had it all wrong. Nothin' good happens when strangers come callin'. Not even strangers with ice cream. So I've put a stop to it. I went down just a while ago and put up a big sign. It says, 'Keep Out.' Nobody's gonna be botherin' us ever again, baby. You don't have to worry 'bout a thing."

Loretta looked down at her little brother snuggled in her arms. It was quiet now, except for the creaking sound of the old wooden rocker. Fast asleep, baby Donald didn't have a care in the world, thanks to Loretta.

★ ★ ★

Loretta "Loretty" Lynn is still one of country music's most beloved entertainers after three decades in the music business. Her first single in 1960, "Honky Tonk Girl," was just the beginning of a long string of *Billboard* and *Cash Box* hits for the young performer. Little did she know back then that she would someday become the most awarded lady in country music. The various awards she has accumulated throughout the years include those from the Country Music Association and TNN Music City News. Loretta holds the distinction of being the first female to receive the Country Music Association's Entertainer of the Year award. She has also earned nine gold albums and has won a GRAMMY.

Loretta's numerous number one hits include some of the most controversial and hard-hitting songs ever recorded by a female country artist: songs with lyrics that have helped women realize their own self-worth. Such well-known Loretta Lynn hits include "The Pill," "One's on the Way," "Don't Come Home a-Drinkin'," "You Ain't Woman Enough to Take My Man," and "Fist City."

One of Clara and Melvin Webb's eight children, Loretta was raised poor in the mountains of Butcher Holler, Kentucky. Part Cherokee Indian, Loretta's mother stayed home to care for the family, and her father worked as a coal miner. Loretta got married when she was just fourteen years old to Oliver "Doolittle" Lynn, began her singing career, and remained happily married until Doolittle's death in 1996. Loretta's younger sister Brenda became a singing success as well under the name Crystal Gayle.

In the mid-1970s, Loretta wrote a best-selling book, *Coal Miner's Daughter,* and a song by the same name, that reflected on her childhood memories, marriage, and early career. Eventually the book was made into a movie, and Loretta became the first country singer with an Oscar-winning biographical film.

Coal Miner's Daughter relates Loretta's humble upbringing and encompasses the stories told here, including the episodes surrounding her "store-boughten dress," and her father's work as a coal miner and his illnesses. Loretta personally related the story of the ice cream for this collection.

Levy Lincoln, Pioneer Man

MARTY STUART

There once was a man named Levy Lincoln, a real-life pioneer man who lived with his wife way out in the country in Philadelphia, Mississippi. Like a character in my adventure books, he was sort of a cross between Daniel Boone and Davy Crockett. People said there weren't many of his kind left, as if he were some prehistoric dinosaur or a specimen you'd study in science class—a perfectly preserved specimen from a whole other place and time.

Some people almost believed that he was just a legend. But Levy Lincoln was definitely living and breathing just like he always had, and he was still as full of life as ever. Like a true-blue, one-of-a-kind hero, with his hands tied behind his back he could outdo and outsmart people half his age—an age that was almost impossible to guess by looking. That's because Levy Lincoln had always been and still was the tallest and strongest man around. A towering figure, he was striking, too, with the thickest, blackest, fullest head of hair that anyone had ever seen—no gray yet. It was much like time had stood still for him. And it actually did stand still where Levy lived.

His house was only nine miles from the town, but it might as well have been one thousand miles in terms of thinking and living. Once you got outside of town and the pavement ended, you just kept driving on a narrow dirt road until you came to the bottom of a little valley. And before you knew it—when you couldn't possibly turn back around—you were suddenly in an earlier time, at a quiet, grassy place. That was Levy Lincoln's house.

Levy lived in an old white house that he'd built all by himself up on the hill. And the first thing you noticed was the long front porch that had bare cedar posts holding everything up. There was a swing at the end, and a big cape jasmine bush and wild roses all around that wrapped you up in the sweetest smell every time the breeze blew. There was also a pond down at the bottom of the hill, a huge oak tree offering shade to the front of the house, and a circular dirt driveway that went down to meet the dirt road.

You'd most likely see Levy, too. Though he didn't ever have a proper job, he was a bona fide Mississippi dirt farmer who worked on his land here and there and was always satisfied with what little he grew to sell and what little he grew to keep. He didn't have any electricity, or running water, or a telephone. Levy lived simply and was content to get everything he could right off his own land without much of anything or anybody to help him.

So it's not surprising that Levy Lincoln had never owned a car or had a reason to learn how to drive. On the rare occasions that he needed to leave his land and go into town for supplies, he would walk unless somebody offered to take him. And that had never been a problem; everybody loved the rough, handsome pioneer.

I thought about Levy Lincoln most of the time. Not only was he one of my heroes, he was also my grandpa, and I called him "Paw." There were a lot of stories about Paw, and I knew them all by heart. But the best one was the story about the car.

★   ★   ★

Yep. Believe it or not, Levy Lincoln had bought a car. A brand-spanking-new 1956 Chevrolet Bel Air. Of all things, nobody ever thought they'd see the day that he would own a car.

"I just got to thinkin' that I wanted to have my own transportation, so I walked to town and bought it myself," Paw had said to me. "What do ya think?"

"Good job, Paw," I said.

It was a special day, and he wanted to make the most of it. Looking out at the new car sitting in the driveway, he squinted his eyes almost like he thought what he was seeing wouldn't be there if he focused better. Then he bent down and looked at the car real good from that way. Then he kind of twisted to the side and craned his neck to catch a look around the other way, too. He was smiling the whole time from ear to ear with the proudest look on his face that I'd ever seen. I wanted to see every possible angle of the car also, so I imitated every move he made. And I smiled, too. In fact, I not only smiled, I jumped up and down with joy and pulled on his sleeve.

Then Paw finally turned to me and said, "All right, partner. Come on inside, and we'll get the key." And in no time flat, we were back outside with the key, getting ready to start the car.

Because it looked so out of place sitting there in Levy Lincoln's dirt driveway, the car was a really big attraction. You'd think it was the very first car ever invented. People from miles around stopped by to see it with their own eyes. They thought it was the craziest thing ever that Paw got a car. But getting the car meant something to me and Paw that people didn't understand. To Paw, who prided himself on being self-reliant, the car meant that he would never be forced to depend on anybody. And to me, it was a sure ticket to new adventures out on the range. Even though my dad owned a car and we drove all the time, Paw's car was special. He would let me get in there alone and pretend that I was driving—something that my parents wouldn't let me do in a million years. They had good reason, though: Mama and Dad hadn't forgotten what happened when I was four.

I remembered it, too. I had been really good that day, and then *BAM!* "What in the world?" my mama was screaming while I was just sitting right in the middle of our living room.

But I hadn't come in the normal way. I'd come in through the window. And in the car, no less. It had only been a minute since I'd climbed into the car in the driveway, when I accidentally knocked it out of gear and ran it through the front of the house. I didn't get hurt, but I absolutely destroyed the front picture window. So Mama declared then that it was hands off the wheel for me.

So neither me nor Paw knew how to drive. But that hadn't stopped us from enjoying every bit of the new car, which just sat there in all its glory. Paw checked the oil in it and cranked it up every day before he drove it once around the circular dirt driveway. You could have walked the driveway in three minutes, but it took him at least ten minutes to putt around the circle in his car to practice driving. Then he stopped it and handed me the key.

It was my turn now, so I took the key and went driving. Well, not really driving. I was happy enough just to sit in it in the driveway. I turned on the radio and listened to music and pretended I was driving to all different kinds of places. And when I got back, I gave the key to Paw and he hid it again under the lid of the piano, where he always kept his important papers and things.

So the car had never strayed from the safety of the dirt circle until one day when my uncle Ralph came by and decided that the three of us would go driving way out in the country. We were going to see somebody about buying some fishing poles. Grandma looked out the front window and just shook her head. She had never liked the car, and she knew Paw still couldn't really drive. "It will be the death of you, Levy Lincoln," she had said repeatedly since it had arrived.

And since she was so scared of the "contraption," as she called it, she especially didn't want me in it. That was in case either Paw or I got a notion to let the other drive once we were out of her sight. Nevertheless, me, Paw, and Uncle Ralph all got into the car and started out slow, with Uncle Ralph driving down the driveway and out the dirt road. Before long all of us were free for miles and miles as we rode through the countryside.

It took a while because we were riding slow and enjoying the scenery, but we finally arrived at Uncle Ralph's friend's house. Paw and Uncle Ralph jumped out and said they'd be right back, and I stayed outside to guard our car. They were gone a long, long time. When they finally came out, they didn't have any fishing poles, and they looked just awful. I asked Paw what was the matter, and he said that before they had gotten around to buying the poles, the friendly man had kindly offered them a sip of his secret, homemade mixture. A secret family recipe known for miles around.

Well, I was glad that I hadn't gone in and been poisoned, because that's for sure what had happened. Paw and Uncle Ralph were sick as dogs. They were so sick that they had to lie down in the car, and Uncle Ralph said I had to drive us all home.

Now, as much as I had wanted to drive the car, this wasn't quite the way I had imagined learning. I was scared to death. But I was more worried that Paw and Uncle Ralph were going to die at any moment, and seeing that there was no other good way I could think of to get us back home, I drove. And it wasn't as easy as it looked.

I was just barely tall enough to reach the pedals and see out of the windshield at the same time. Even though I had watched Uncle Ralph drive the car, I didn't have the faintest idea how to shift the gears around. So I just left the gear lever in the first slot, and as we started out, Paw's car sputtered and lurched at a snail's pace.

All the country dirt roads looked pretty much the same, so thank goodness I sort of knew my way around. I had always liked to know where everybody lived and everybody's name and their dog's name and whose kids were whose. And that sure came in handy now. As the car chugged slowly, I figured that we had gone about ten miles away from home, judging by familiar things along the way. And those were the longest ten miles of my life. It seemed like it took forever for me to get us back safely.

Right before we got to Paw's house, Uncle Ralph raised up and said, "You'd better pull over and let me do the driving up to the house so your grandma won't know." So we switched places and drove right in like nothing was the matter. Maw was waiting for us at the door. I was still really scared, and every time I got nervous my face got red. That's all it took. Maw took one look at them and one look at me and knew exactly what had happened.

But she still turned to me and said, "Doc"—she always called me Doc—"what have you been doing?"

"Nothing, Maw. Nothing," I said. "I promise I didn't drive the car."

Well, she left the room so fast, it would make your head spin, and I heard her close the door and really let Paw and Uncle Ralph have it. Then she came back and put me in her lap and said, "Baby, are you all right?"

And I said, "Yes, ma'am. I'm fine."

That was the last driving that me and Paw's car ever did. It took days before Paw was well, so I think the whole incident scared him now as much as it had scared me then. It was easy for Maw to convince him that the car would be the absolute death of him if he

didn't leave it alone. "Things like those dangerous contraptions are what come along and ruin good people like you, Levy Lincoln," she said.

And maybe she was right. Paw and I went back to fishing and hunting and telling stories together. And the car just sat and rested in the driveway for me to use for sitting and dreaming and listening to the radio whenever I wanted. Deep down, I knew it would be all right with Paw if I took it when I got my license. But I had already decided that it should always stay right where it was. It was a part of Levy Lincoln's story. A story that should never be forgotten.

★ ★ ★

Marty Stuart has made a special contribution to the world of country music for the past twenty-eight years. A Mississippi native, he was only thirteen when he landed a job in Lester Flatt's bluegrass band as a result of his mandolin playing. From there he played with fiddler Vassar Clements and acoustic guitar great Doc Watson before he played with the country legend Johnny Cash for six years. Finally, Marty signed a recording contract with Columbia Records and had his first top twenty hit with "Arlene" in 1985.

Two gold albums later and after a string of hit singles with MCA, Marty's 1992 duet with Travis Tritt, "The Whiskey Ain't Workin'," earned him a GRAMMY Award. And that same year, he realized a lifelong dream: He became a member of the Grand Ole Opry.

Now with a total of three GRAMMY Awards and four gold albums, Marty is by no means just a singer. He's assembled what could be the largest collection of country music memorabilia in the world; he's the president of the Country Music Foundation; he was the executive producer of music for *The Hi-Lo Country,* a film starring Woody Harrelson; and he's begun writing a short story collection. Marty also scored the music for Billy Bob Thornton's movie *Daddy and Them,* and Rutledge Hill Press recently published Marty's first book, *Pilgrims: Sinners, Saints, and Prophets,* "a book of words and photographs."

This particular tale is the true story of his grandfather, Levy Lincoln Stuart. Marty overflows with a wealth of details as he recalls this story, and he maintains that those times with his Paw were some of the best in his life, down to the smell of the cape jasmine bush that he still distinctly remembers. Marty says that his grandma and grandpa finally got running water, but they never had a telephone. And when asked if the 1956 Chevrolet Bel Air is still around, Marty says that it burned up one day and nobody ever really figured out how. "Probably for the best, though," he says, laughing.

Dreams

LeAnn Rimes

Everybody in Pelahatchie, Mississippi, had been gearing up for weeks for the annual Little Miss Pelahatchie Pageant. Held on the Fourth of July, it was a fun-filled, down-home affair, and the whole town came out for it. There were pie contests and potluck suppers, a minicarnival, and a big square dance—all leading up to pageant night. And then, once the winner was announced, there was a huge fireworks show and a winner's parade around the main square. Everyone would cheer and cheer, waving flags and congratulating the newly crowned Little Miss Pelahatchie.

Young ladies ages ten to twelve could participate in the pageant, and most all of the girls who grew up there wanted to win the contest as soon as they were eligible to participate—particularly Ann. She had recently celebrated her tenth birthday, and winning the Little Miss Pelahatchie Pageant had always been her dream. And even though there was a large number of very promising entries this year, many of the townspeople were already predicting that Ann would win the title. A town darling, Ann did well in school, volunteered for all the community projects, and played softball. Not to mention that she was quite a little talent.

Ever since Ann had been three years old, she had taken dance from Miss Kim, and she loved it. No one could forget the kindergarten play years ago with little Ann standing there in a blue-and-white dress that her mother had made especially for her. Tapping and singing away, she didn't miss a beat, even that young. Ann was practically a shoo-in for the pageant title this year. That is until Alexandra Thompson showed up.

"My given name is Alexandra, not Alex," she announced to everyone when she swept into town just a few months ago with her family.

Her father had been transferred midyear to some big job nearby, and her mother's lifework was dedicated to grooming Alexandra, which became quite apparent when she squealed with delight upon learning of the upcoming Little Miss Pelahatchie Pageant. Everyone hoped that Alexandra wasn't an insufferable, selfish brat. But they could have hoped forever. The pageant's worst nightmare had officially arrived.

Her first day in Ann's class, Alexandra showed up wearing a floofy pink dress complete with shiny white patent-leather shoes with turned-down, triple-lace socks and a silver-colored, plastic-coated crown. Ann could have sworn that Alexandra's perfect bun was permanently hair-sprayed on the top of her head, not to mention her too rosy cheeks that were clearly the result of makeup.

"How in the world does she expect to play ball in that getup?" Ann wondered out loud.

"I don't play childish games," Alexandra had announced to her classmates right away. "I have a pageant coach, and I must make time for my rehearsals each and every afternoon. That's so I'll win, just like I always do. And especially in wherever-we-are-Mississippi, my mother said it would be a cinch. But maybe you girls would like to come by my house sometime. If you're quiet, I'll show you all of my costumes."

Of course Alexandra wasn't ever this bossy or vain in front of the teacher. She was respectful and sugary sweet right off the bat, and the teacher admired her poise and complimented her dedication and seriousness. And ironically, all the girls were fascinated with Alexandra's grown-up demeanor. They had never seen anyone quite like her, much less someone their own age. Not to mention they wanted a glimpse of her fancy costumes and to hear all about a real-life pageant coach.

But not Ann. She didn't want to go to Alexandra's. She thought she was different, all right. Different and awful. And she felt sure that Alexandra was just making things up. Nobody had a pageant coach, for goodness' sake. All the other girls would see soon enough.

★　★　★

"Ann, you were completely wrong," her best friend, Laura, said the next day. "Alexandra had the loveliest all-pink room that I've ever seen, complete with a vanity set all the way from Paris and a huge walk-in closet full of beautiful costume after beautiful costume. And her mother even said herself that Alexandra did have a pageant coach, and then she told us all about Alexandra's act. It all sounds really, really fantastic."

According to Laura, Alexandra intended to sing "I'm a Yankee Doodle Dandy" in a one-of-a-kind red-white-and-blue-sequined leotard. And that wasn't all. Alexandra was actually going to ride a pony—a real live pony that her dad was going to have sent over just for the show. Absolutely incredible, all the girls had agreed. There was no doubt that she was going to steal the show.

Ann's heart sank. She had always dreamed about winning the Little Miss Pelahatchie Pageant, and now she would never have a chance. She didn't have a pony. She didn't have a sequined outfit. She didn't have a pageant coach. Suddenly, she felt plain and unprepared. Who cared about the silly old Little Miss Pelahatchie Pageant, anyway? She didn't.

"I don't want to be in the pageant," Ann announced to her mother when she arrived home from school that afternoon. "Alexandra is going to win hands down. She has a special coach and a fancy costume. I'll never win, and I don't care, anyway. It's a stupid contest." Ann sat down quietly on the front steps, exhausted from disappointment.

"Now, Ann," her mother consoled. "That's the most ridiculous thing I've ever heard in my entire life. Why, being in the pageant has been one of your dreams. You've worked hard, and you are very, very good. No costume or pony or anything else can replace your talent and your heart. You'd do best to quit worrying about everyone else and just do what you do best."

"That's what all mothers think," Ann mumbled. "But how can I compete with a pony? Much less a pony with a coach?"

Still sitting on her front steps, tears slowly running down her cheeks, Ann stared blankly at the bait shop across the street. Maybe she'd just sit there for the rest of her life, or at least until the pageant was over. And finally laying her head sleepily against the wooden railing, she dreamed of life before Alexandra. A wonderful life . . . and then she saw her: A woman was walking toward her from the direction of the bait shop. And she wasn't any regular woman. She was a genuine pageant coach. It said so, right on her big tapestry suitcase.

Ann couldn't believe it. "Boy, am I glad to see you. You're just in time," Ann said, and hopped up in excitement. "How in the world did my mother find you?"

"I don't have any idea what you are talking about, and nobody found me. I have obviously found you. My name is Mrs. Chaney, and I presume that you are Ann," the woman said, reading from a little card that she had pulled quickly out of her bag. "And I'm perfectly aware that we must get down to business, is that right?" Mrs. Chaney said, barely taking a breath.

"Why, yes," Ann answered in amazement.

"Well, then, what seems to be your problem with the pageant? Is it your voice you're worried about?"

"No, ma'am," Ann responded. "I think my voice is just fine."

"Well, then," the woman continued, "is it your dancing that's a problem?"

"No, ma'am," Ann responded. "Miss Kim has made sure I know my dances very well."

"Then, my heavens, I must have gotten my wires crossed, because you certainly don't need me," Mrs. Chaney concluded, and turned to leave.

"Oh, but Mrs. Chaney," Ann pleaded, "I do need your help." And with that, Ann told her the whole story about Alexandra and her coach and her outfits and her pony. "I can't possibly win if I don't have things like that. She'll steal the show." Ann plopped down wearily once again.

"And do you really believe that if you had something like a pony or a special costume, you'd win?"

"Oh, I'm sure of it," Ann said.

"Well, then, if that's the case, I may be able to help you after all," Mrs. Chaney said, reaching down deep into her bag and pulling out a dog. And not just a regular dog: It was a dog dressed in a tutu.

As if pulling a dog with a tutu out of her bag was the most ordinary thing in the world, Mrs. Chaney announced, "Meet Mercedes. She is the most famous show dog in the entire world. She can dance and twirl and jump through hoops. So, of course, you'd be sure to win with Mercedes at your side. That is, if you follow the rules. She is a very special dog, and I rarely lend her to anyone, only in those few rare cases that I consider to be emergencies."

"Oh, Mrs. Chaney," Ann begged. "This is an emergency. And I promise that I'll follow the rules. Please, please let Mercedes be my partner in the pageant. I promise that I'll take care of her. You won't be sorry."

Mrs. Chaney looked from Ann to Mercedes, who was already practicing her dog pirouettes in the front yard. "Okay, then. Listen closely," Mrs. Chaney said, crouching close to Ann and whispering low. "First of all, Mercedes doesn't like sequins and things like that. They distract her. So you'll need to wear just what your mother has made for you. It's perfect. Second of all, you can't look over at Mercedes during the show. You have to concentrate on what you do best, looking right out at the audience, and let Mercedes handle the rest. And if you should glance over, Mercedes will start howling something terrible, and your entire show will be ruined. Sadly, I've seen it happen many, many times."

"But, Mrs. Chaney," Ann asked, "how are we supposed to do our act together if I can't look at Mercedes?"

"You leave that to me and Mercedes. She'll know just what to do, don't you worry. I'll bring her there right as you're going on. And you'll win. Just remember, no peeking."

Ann's mother was standing at the front door and interrupted her. "Ann, this is the last time I'm going to ask you to quit moping on those steps. It's time to get ready for the pageant." Ann was startled and jumped up from her resting place. Mrs. Chaney was nowhere in sight, and neither was Mercedes. "She sure left in a hurry," Ann said to her mother.

"Who left in a hurry?" her mother asked.

"Why, Mrs. Chaney, of course. And thank you so much for everything. She was wonderful. And she agreed, just like I told you, that I needed some help in the pageant. I can hardly wait," Ann said excitedly.

"Whoever Mrs. Chaney is, I have no earthly idea. And right now I don't have time to find out," Ann's mother replied. "I'm just glad that you've quit worrying about Alexandra and the pageant. Now, hurry up and get ready or you're going to be late."

★　★　★

The next several hours were a blur. Ann arrived in a pretty blue-and-white dress, much like the one she'd worn in the kindergarten play years ago. Standing backstage, Ann saw that her outfit paled next to Alexandra's patriotic sequins, but Ann didn't care. She had Mercedes in her back pocket. The white Arabian pony standing at the bottom of the backstage stairs did nothing to shake her confidence. She even had the graciousness to pet his nose and wish Alexandra good luck.

"Oh, I won't be the one who needs luck," Alexandra quipped.

The lineup of expectant Little Miss Pelahatchies was long. Cynthia went first and played the piano beautifully. The selection was one of Clementi's sonatinas, and she didn't miss a note. Betsy went second, twirling the baton and never dropping it. She was even able to catch it behind her back several times. The competition was proving to be quite stiff, and it was already apparent that the judges were going to have a hard time picking only one winner. Fine performances kept coming one after the other.

"We only have two performances left," the emcee announced. Ann was second to last, and Alexandra was last. And even though the lineup had been drawn from a hat earlier in the day, Alexandra was sure that her placement was arranged purposely.

"They always save the best for last," Alexandra announced loudly as Ann prepared to go onstage.

Ann hadn't seen Mrs. Chaney or Mercedes, but of course she knew that she wouldn't. That was the rule. She'd see them afterward. So, ignoring Alexandra's self-centered comments, Ann happily stepped out on the stage when it was her turn. She paused for a moment, and even though she wouldn't dare look, she could feel Mercedes next to her. She could do it. She could win. And, staring straight into the audience, Ann sang "Getting to Know You." The strength and beauty of her voice and the accuracy of her difficult dance maneuvers belied Ann's age. Her feet tapped in perfect rhythm as she imagined herself singing this very song in *The King and I* on Broadway one day. She was singing from the bottom of her heart, with every ounce of effort she had. Everyone kept cheering and cheering when she finished. As Ann exited the stage, glowing, it was one of her proudest moments. No matter what happened, she knew that she had done the very best she could.

"Hmmpf," Alexandra snipped as the other contestants waiting backstage congratulated Ann on a good job. "Watch closely now, girls. All of you amateurs are going to see a real pro."

Alexandra was the only contestant left. People were sitting up on the edge of their seat just waiting for the grand finale. But Alexandra didn't appear right away. There was some sort of commotion happening backstage. And as it got louder and louder, everyone in the audience could hear exactly what was being said.

"What do you mean he won't do it?" Alexandra was shouting. "Get that nasty animal up here before I scream."

The pony wouldn't go up the stage steps, even with Alexandra and her parents frantically pushing it from behind. Her mother was screaming at her father. Her father was screaming at her mother. Alexandra was screaming at both of them, and they were all screaming at the pony.

"Give me the reins now!" Alexandra bellowed. As she grabbed them, she slipped and tore her sequined outfit in the process. Her "permanent" bun tumbled down in defeat, and the pony escaped through the open backstage door.

"See what you've made me do!" Alexandra pointed at the director.

"Come on now and just perform your song-and-dance routine. The horse doesn't matter," the director said as soothingly as he could under the circumstances.

"But it's my act," Alexandra yelled. "A very well-planned act with the horse and the outfit. An act that was sure to win. I demand that the contest be postponed until I'm ready," Alexandra continued as she lay down on the floor and starting kicking her feet.

"I'm sorry, Alexandra," the director stated matter-of-factly. "The pageant will not be delayed any longer. You are disqualified for bad sportsmanship."

The audience gasped in horror at hearing the entire exchange as the director walked onstage and calmly announced that the final performance had been cancelled. No further explanation was needed. Poor little spoiled-rotten Alexandra had missed the whole point of the pageant.

The judges began their deliberations. It was obviously not going to be an easy choice. The air was tense backstage as the contestants waited to hear. The audience waited quietly. Minute after minute the anticipation built until finally the director walked to the podium. "Ladies and gentlemen," he began. "This has been one of our closest contests ever, and I'm sure you'll agree that all of our fine entries are winners here tonight. But there can be only one Little Miss Pelahatchie. And this year, the title goes to contestant number fourteen, for 'Getting to Know You.'"

Ann could hardly believe her ears. She had done her very best, and she had won! Her dream had finally come true. With tears of happiness streaming down her rosy cheeks, and clutching a small bouquet of red roses, Ann was crowned Little Miss Pelahatchie.

"I've just got to thank Mrs. Chaney and Mercedes," Ann said to those gathered around afterward backstage. "Has anyone seen them?" she asked, describing the pair and their part in her winning.

Nobody seemed to know what she was talking about.

"I didn't see any dog on the stage," someone said.

"A dog in a tutu? I've never heard of such a thing, much less seen one," another person said.

"You were there all by yourself, and boy did you do good," she heard someone else say.

"Excuse me," Ann's mother said to the gathered crowd as she reached over and hugged Ann. "Ann must just be overwhelmed with happiness. She's been imagining things all day."

Ann was puzzled. Mrs. Chaney and Mercedes had been to her house. Mercedes had been in the show. She was sure it was true.

The evening's celebration finally ended with a

spectacular display of red, white, and blue shooting stars. And after basking in the warmth of everyone's heartfelt congratulations, Ann strolled home arm-in-arm with her parents and went straight up to bed. It had been a long day, and she was very, very tired.

Poking her head in the doorway, her mother said, "We're so proud of you, Ann. I knew all along you could do it, as long as you believed in yourself and your dreams. Good night, Little Miss Pelahatchie."

Alone now and glancing out her bedroom window as she prepared to climb into bed, Ann thought she saw Mrs. Chaney and Mercedes waving good-bye and dancing away toward the bait shop in the moonlight.

✦　✦　✦

LeAnn Rimes's love of music began very early. An only child born in Jackson, Mississippi, she began singing before she was two. At age five, LeAnn won her first song-and-dance competition, singing a version of "Getting to Know You." She recalls knowing then that she wanted to be in show business.

LeAnn and her parents, Wilbur and Belinda, moved to Texas when she was just six, and there, at age seven, she made her stage debut playing the lead role of Tiny Tim in a Dallas musical production of *A Christmas Carol.* LeAnn was also a two-week champion on the *Star Search* television show at age eight and was a regular on *Johnnie High's Country Music Review* in Fort Worth.

Her first album, at age eleven, entitled *All That,* was produced by her father and featured a version of the now-famous song "Blue." The song was soon rerecorded, and LeAnn signed a recording contract with Curb Records. Her first CD was *Blue,* which became a multiplatinum seller, followed by *You Light Up My Life: Inspirational Songs,* and *Unchained Melody: The Early Years,* also multiplatinum-selling records. The single "Unchained Melody" successfully crossed over into the pop charts, as did the number one pop-selling hit "How Do I Live." Next, her 1998 album *Sittin' on Top of the World* featured the hit single "Commitment," as well as "Looking Through Your Eyes"—a ballad included in the animated motion picture *Quest for Camelot.* And in 1999 LeAnn performed "Written in the Stars," a duet with Elton John from his and Tim Rice's *Aida* album. Her latest album, entitled *LeAnn Rimes,* features her unique interpretations of eleven country standards. For these recording accomplishments, LeAnn has been named a winner at the American Music

Awards, GRAMMY Awards, TNN Music City News Awards, CMA Awards, and the *Billboard* Music Awards.

In addition to recording hit records, LeAnn coauthored a book with Tom Carter about her life, *Holiday in Your Heart.* It was followed by her first starring television role in *ABC's Movie of the Week* under the same title.

LeAnn remembers her days dancing and singing in Pelahatchie, Mississippi. Miss Kim, her dance teacher, helped prepare her for the contests she would enter early on, and LeAnn fondly describes Mrs. Chaney not only as her elementary school teacher but also as her encourager and best friend. The family lived across from a bait shop, and after much begging, LeAnn got Mercedes—a dog given to her by a family who was moving out of town.

The Magic Guitar

GEORGE JONES

Clad in overalls, Glen was a familiar sight. He walked back and forth, up and down the streets, and all the while, he sang and played the magic guitar that he kept slung over his back. Or at least he said it was magic. And that was a big part of the mystery.

At first, Glen and his family didn't seem any different from any of the other families in Beaumont, Texas. Most all of us moved here from the country into a new complex of two-story apartments that the government built. All in all, more than six hundred families lived here, right next to one another, so it was hard not to know everybody's business. And considering that Glen was my best friend, I thought I pretty much knew everything there was to know about him.

He had eight brothers and sisters, but he and his sister Doris were the only ones who still lived at home. Nobody knew much of anything about his dad other than he worked mostly in the shipyard and in other places, too. He was hardly ever home, to the point where few people had ever seen him. It was almost like he didn't exist at all, but since a lot of the dads went off working for long stretches, nobody thought much about it for the time being. "Probably just a jack-of-all-trades and a master of none," I sometimes heard my dad say. But it didn't much matter. Glen's mother had more than enough love to go around when his dad wasn't home.

She was one of the nicest ladies around, with one of the prettiest voices you've ever heard. And she was always happy. At night, we could hear her singing clear through the walls, and during the day, she spent her time doting on Glen and finding someone who needed helping. Otherwise, you could find her at church, where she faithfully played the organ every Sunday. "Just like an angel," my mother said, and I agreed. She had to be an angel to put up with Glen.

Like most of us eleven-year-olds, Glen was always into something, and most of the time he'd talk me into going with him. He would pull one of his favorite pranks at his brother Herman's house. Herman and his wife, Evalina, lived outside of town, almost in the country. And Glen knew that when Herman was at work, Evalina was always in a state. Even though no one had ever done her any harm, she was scared to death of the hoboes. They would jump off the trains that ran right behind her house and would come knocking on her door, wanting whatever she'd be willing to give them. They weren't looking for any trouble, but she'd scream and run and hide, anyway, until they left, which they all did pretty quickly. I think she scared them more than they scared her. Except, of course, when Glen and I came around.

Glen would sneak around the back of the house, start moaning kind of low, and bang up and down on the door and scratch a long stick across the screen for the longest time, until Evalina was so beside herself that she'd almost faint from fear. Then Glen would laugh and laugh, and once Evalina figured out that it was us, she would get so mad that she'd chase us all the way to the end of the dirt road, screaming and hollering the whole way. We'd run all the way home and collapse on the ground outside the apartments, laughing until our sides hurt and until we decided what else to do.

And that's pretty much the way it went, me and Glen playing together day after day. But then came the time not long ago that everything suddenly changed, and that's when the mystery began.

It all started when some people noticed Glen's dad walking through town. No one saw what direction he'd come from; he was just kind of there all of a sudden. A tall, strong-looking man with a kindly face, he never looked around or waved or smiled at anybody. He just stared straight ahead down the road. And he was carrying, of all things, a shiny new little guitar that shimmered in the sunlight and kind of glowed. I'm not sure why—maybe because of the glowing—but everybody got quiet and stood still, making room for him to pass by and watching him the whole way until he disappeared into the door of his apartment.

Even though you couldn't hear it, the sound of the door closing seemed to jolt everybody out of their trance, and they gradually went back to their business. But not me. I headed straight for Glen's house. I figured the small guitar had to be for him, and even though I knew he couldn't possibly know how to play it yet, I still couldn't wait to see that shiny guitar up close.

When I got there, Glen was sitting by himself, holding the guitar. "Wow," I said. "That's something else, Glen. And it isn't even your birthday or anything. What's the occasion? What made your dad decide to get you that guitar?"

Glen looked up at me and said, "What? My dad didn't buy me this guitar. He's not here and won't be coming back again for a while. He's working."

"But, Glen," I said, "I saw your dad walking through town with that guitar. A lot of people saw him. We even saw him come into your house a few minutes ago. I just wondered where he bought it and if you're going to learn to play it. It's one of the prettiest guitars I've ever seen."

And as serious as he could be—kind of grown-up-sounding for an eleven-year-old like me—he waited a second and said, "My dad didn't buy me this guitar, and he didn't give it to me, either. This is a magic guitar. You can't buy magic guitars. And nobody can give them to you. You can't find them, either. Magic guitars find you."

"Yeah, right," I said. "Quit joking, Glen. Let me see it." But Glen wouldn't let go, and he wouldn't talk to me anymore, either.

So, okay. Now I was mad. I was steaming mad. Glen had ridden my new birthday bike around and around, and I hadn't cared. After all, we were best friends.

"Glen, I let you ride my new bike all you wanted, and I never said a thing," I told him. "The least you could do is let me just hold your new guitar. I'm not going to hurt it."

"I said no," Glen said. "Now, go on and leave me alone. I'm not going to talk about it anymore."

I begged a few more times, but he still wouldn't tell me where his dad got the guitar, and he still wouldn't let me hold it. It was unbelievable.

"Fine, Glen," I said. "You and your guitar can just stay here by yourselves. I'm leaving,

and it'll be a long time before I come back. And don't ever ask to ride my bike again. Do you hear me?"

Glen didn't answer, which infuriated me even more. I left in a huff and slammed the door behind me. Deep down inside, I knew that Glen would come to his senses tomorrow.

Or so I thought. But strange things started happening the next day and the next and the next. Glen hopped out of his door the very next morning, and from that point on, the magic guitar was the only thing he cared about. But the most amazing thing was that Glen had somehow learned to play it overnight. He could sing and play that guitar like nobody you've ever heard, big or little. He just sang and strummed up a storm.

Crowds would gather around wherever he went. They loved it, and it was clear that Glen loved it, too. He'd go to the fire hall and sing and joke with the firemen awhile, or he'd get on one of the city buses and go to the very back and play and sing for all the people riding. All the bus drivers knew about him and his magic guitar by now, so they'd let him ride at no charge. He'd ride from one end of town to the other and then get off and catch another one, singing and playing as loud as he could the whole time.

★ ★ ★

One evening when he was sitting on the shoe-shine stand downtown all by himself—playing and singing, of course—passersby going to the movies stopped to listen as usual. But this time they did something different. They started throwing nickels and dimes on the concrete, and before it was all over, Glen had ten dollars—more than any of us kids had ever seen. And besides that, none of us had imagined that Glen could get money from the magic guitar. I don't think he had, either. It's like it confused him for a moment, but in a split second, Glen had it all worked out. When he finally quit singing, he would spend every dime of it on himself, playing games in the arcade. A dream come true.

That's about when all the neighborhood kids decided that the guitar was magic beyond a shadow of a doubt—just like Glen said—and that made every one of us really jealous of him. It wasn't only because of the attention and money Glen got. We were mostly envious of his mysterious ability to play that guitar and sing so well. So we all decided that we would figure out a way to get Glen's guitar. Not take it from him, but get it and hold it to see if maybe, just maybe, the magic would rub off on us. And then if it worked, we'd find out where Glen's dad got it, so we could each get one, too.

The problem with this plan was that Glen wouldn't let anyone have his guitar, and he never put it down. Some of the guys whispered that he would even hold it while he was asleep. It went with him everywhere, except of course when Glen came to school. He absolutely wasn't allowed to take his guitar to school. Even if he could, there was no good place to put it so that nobody would take it, and the teachers certainly wouldn't let him hold it during class. It would have made writing and thinking a little too hard for all of us. I'm sure that's one of the reasons Glen left school every day right when the final bell rang, and headed straight for the woods.

The part of Texas that we lived in wasn't all flat and sort of empty like the other parts. Of course there were flat places, but we also had some woods with big, tall pine trees, and all other kinds of trees bending down. We would walk to school together every day from the apartments, and to get there we had to walk right through a patch of the woods. It wasn't a big forest or anything, but it was big enough to get a little lost in if you wanted. That's where Glen stayed a lot of the time. He would go into the woods all by himself to sing and play, and so we thought that's where he hid the guitar when he came to school.

Actually, we didn't think it; we *knew* it. That's because one day we saw him scrambling around and pulling the magic guitar out from under a bunch of leaves. But since then we hadn't been able to find out exactly where the guitar was. One of the boys even sneaked out of class one day and went hunting all over the woods for it, but he never found it. And the times that it rained, and we knew the magic guitar was hiding in the woods, we were sure it had been ruined with water and could never be played again. But even with the biggest storms you could imagine, the magic guitar and Glen would always show up somewhere, playing as good as ever.

It was driving us all crazy. No matter how hard we tried, it appeared as if we would never solve the mystery of the magic guitar. Glen was still holding tight to the guitar and was singing and playing anywhere and everywhere, and no one had seen his dad since the day the magic guitar had come to town. And just when we were about to give up, it happened on one dark night: We found Glen's dad.

One night, several of us kids were playing ball in front of our apartment complex after dusk, and we heard Glen singing and playing his guitar really loud. Normally we didn't hear him at night, so we automatically looked up into his window, and there he was. But someone else was there, too, and it wasn't his mother or Doris. It was his dad. Or at least it *looked* like his dad, for all we could remember. And he was playing, too: dancing a jig in the shadows of the window, and playing a guitar as well. Or was he playing a harmonica? Or was he playing them both at the same time? We weren't sure, but Glen was singing better than ever. And then, in a flash, Glen's dad wasn't there in the window anymore. It was just Glen, and his single voice faded off about the time we had to go in for the night.

None of us slept that night. We were going first thing the next morning to talk to Glen's dad and finally find out about the magic guitar. But as it turned out, nobody was at their house. We couldn't find Glen or his mother or his dad anywhere. We thought for sure that we were right on the verge of solving the mystery. But, like always, we came up empty-handed.

"I know," I said. And I didn't know why I hadn't thought of it before. "We'll go talk to Sister Annie Stephens. She's Glen's Sunday school teacher, and she knows Glen's family better than anybody. She'll give it to us straight, I'm sure of it," I said.

So we all marched down to Sister Annie Stephens's house, on the edge of town. It was a grand moment, the moment we knew that we would solve the mystery. The moment that we would all be able to get a magic guitar. The moment we had all been waiting for.

Sister Annie Stephens didn't seem the least bit surprised to see us standing in the doorway—it was almost like she'd been waiting—and she quickly invited us into her small but cozy house. We all sat down in a row, and she said, "Now. To what do I owe the pleasure of this special visit from such a handsome group?"

I don't know who spoke first, because we were all talking a mile a minute at the same time.

"Now, slow down, all of you," she said. "Let's just one of you try to tell me what in the world is going on."

As Glen's best friend, I spoke up. "Sister Annie," I said, "we just have to know where Glen's dad got that magic guitar—you must know it's magic—'cause we all want one, too. So please, please. We feel sure you know. Please help us find out about the magic guitar."

Sister Annie Stephens rubbed her hands on her apron, looked each one of us right in the eye, and said, "Oh my goodness gracious, no. You must be mistaken. Glen's daddy hasn't been home for months. And when it comes to a magic guitar, why, all of you know that can't be true. Guitars aren't magic. Surely you know that."

"But, Sister Annie," we interrupted in unison, "Glen said his guitar *is* magic, and we've seen the special things it can do. There's no mistaking that it's magic."

"Well, well." She sighed. "I guess, then, that Glen doesn't even know it himself yet. But he's the one who's magic. Magic inside and out."

And with that, she spun around and left the room. She left us all sitting there with our mouths wide open. Sister Annie had said that Glen himself was magic. But, how?

Oh, no, we all thought. Back to square one. We had a whole new mystery to figure out.

★ ★ ★

George Glen Jones was born in Saratoga, Texas, and spent most of his childhood living in nearby Beaumont and singing for tips on the streets. By the time he was twenty-four years old, he had already been married, served in the marines, and was an experienced singer and guitar player on the Texas honky-tonk music circuit.

George's first hit, "Why, Baby, Why," topped the charts in the 1950s, and from there he has enjoyed one hit single after another in every decade since. In the 1980s he recorded "He Stopped Loving Her Today," which has proved to be one of the all-time great country records, and in 1992 George was elected to the Country Music Hall of Fame. He told his life story in the 1996 book *I Lived to Tell It All*, which went to number six on *The New York Times* Best-seller List. One of his latest CDs, *Cold Hard Truth* on Asylum Records, shows why George is often acclaimed as the very definition of country music.

When George was a child, his father walked him downtown one day and bought him a little guitar. From that time on, George never stopped playing and singing. He sang in the church and went on church revivals with Sister Annie Stephens and her husband. His sister Doris sang well also, and their dad loved to hear them sing hymns together at night at home. George did sing on various corners in town, where, much to his delight, people threw money down, and he'd go spend the rest of the afternoon in the penny arcade. George chuckles as he tells about riding the bus for free from one end of town to the other, and about hiding his guitar under the leaves in the woods. He really did carry it everywhere with him, and even though most guitars would likely be ruined with the least bit of water, for some reason George's guitar survived downpour after downpour.

Follow the Yellow Brick Road

TRISHA YEARWOOD

Patricia had the best seat in the house, which is a hard thing to get in Hollywood, or so she'd been told. But there she was, absolutely mesmerized, staring right at a real-life movie star. Rita Hayworth looked beautiful gliding down the grand spiral staircase, wearing long evening gloves, with her hair swept up in a diamond clip. Her close-fitting ivory silk dress puddled a bit on the steps behind her, then delicately turned up at her ankles to reveal lovely gold slippers as she walked. She was the most glamorous actress Patricia had ever seen, and Patricia decided then and there that she wanted to be a glamorous star, too. Hopefully another great old movie would be on tomorrow afternoon.

Sitting in front of the television was about the closest that Patricia was going to get to Hollywood, seemingly a world away.

It had been a normal day in small-town America, and nobody seemed to mind, except Patricia. She wasn't normal. She was different. Or rather she felt different. Kind of like trying to fit a square peg in a round hole, Patricia always knew that she was meant to do something extraordinary but she hadn't quite figured out what or how. That is, until the afternoon she had stepped into the house and discovered that Rita Hayworth was there.

Every afternoon, Patricia hopped off the school bus at 3 P.M. and clambered up the front steps of her family's brick home. Neither her big sister nor her parents would be home yet. But no one ever bothered anyone in Monticello, Georgia, and everybody always left their doors unlocked day and night. Enveloped by the surrounding thirty acres and grazing cattle, Patricia felt safe as always and looked forward to a couple of hours of uninterrupted fun.

Most of the ten-year-olds played softball after school, so that's what Patricia did every afternoon, too. The schedule hardly ever changed. So from school, to ball, to bed, Patricia

had no real concept of the world outside Monticello, except through the television, which she rarely sat down and watched other than an occasional episode of *Family Affair* or *The Brady Bunch.* Those were her favorites. So it was completely out of the ordinary on that typical afternoon that Patricia turned on the TV while getting ready to go out to play ball. And it was even more extraordinary that it made her stop in her tracks. Patricia just stood there, frozen, glued to the television by the remaining half of an old black-and-white Rita Hayworth movie. She couldn't have cared less about playing ball that day. Patricia had discovered her life's calling.

She ran right upstairs to her room, stood in front of her mirror, and imitated the way Rita Hayworth had held her head, batted her eyelashes, and waved her jeweled hand ever so slightly. Besides the apparent differences—age being the main one—Patricia wasn't half bad. She just needed some practice and a few props. And by the time her family arrived home that evening, Patricia had been reincarnated.

Her sister, Beth, and her mom and dad arrived home about the same time. "We're home, Patricia," everybody yelled.

"Patricia, dear, where are you?" her mother called again upstairs.

"Good evening," Patricia said in the huskiest voice she could muster, and they all looked up in surprise. Patricia was posed at the top of the stairs, waiting to make her grand entrance. Wearing her mother's long, fuzzy pink bathrobe while teetering in a pair of oversized high-heeled shoes, and wearing a piece of satin ribbon tied up in her short hair, Patricia was a darling sight.

"Now, what do we have here?" her dad asked, chuckling.

"Are you actually playing dress-up?" her sister teased.

"Why, I don't have the faintest idea of who you are talking about," Patricia purred as she glided down the stairs. "I'm one of the most famous movie stars in the world, and I'm completely charmed that you darlings have all welcomed me so graciously into your home."

"Well, well." Patricia's mother smiled. "Would Miss Movie Star be so kind as to return the favor by helping us in with the groceries?" And with that, everybody went about their evening chores, shaking their head in amusement.

But Patricia wasn't joking. Every day after school, she plopped in front of the television set to watch old movies and musicals. And she realized right away that she needed lots of practice to prepare for the day when she would head for the big city. As a star, she'd be assured the best seat in the house. So, with that in mind, Patricia would skip up to her room for rehearsal. She had stashed her stuffed animals away, along with her softball mitt, and replaced them with a small radio and a long-handled brush that served as her microphone. And there, in front of her dresser mirror, Patricia would happily sing along with the radio for the longest time and practice movie scenes, complete with commercials.

By now, Patricia had told everyone in town about her big-city dreams, and they all indulged her fantasies. It was hard not to. All the neighbors played along when Patricia rang their bells, posing as an Avon lady to collect money for her upcoming trip. Some would even go so far as to purchase her "exclusive" line of beauty products, which they knew consisted only of her mother's old fingernail polish and cracked face powder. And her mom and dad would let her sing songs and perform skits not only for them but also when they had friends over for dinner. They had no idea where her spunkiness had come from or who had put these wild ideas into her head about going to the big city. But they couldn't deny that she was actually very good, and as a result, everyone was entertained night after night.

★　★　★

Once Patricia had mastered Rita Hayworth's style and had perfected her singing voice, her favorite thing to do was to impersonate Cher. Cher had recently made her glamorous television debut, and after watching her, Patricia had decided that she wanted to be like Cher more than anything in the whole wide world. That's all she talked about. Patricia felt sure that if she could just sing and look like her, she would be on her way to the big city.

At this point, singing wasn't necessarily the problem. It was looking like Cher that was the hard part. And to Patricia, the primary consideration was Cher's waist-length black hair, which of course looked nothing like her own. Patricia's hair was blond and short. Her mother had cut it the same way for years and years. First, she'd keep the bottom trimmed up in a short bowl shape. Then she'd put a piece of tape across Patricia's forehead so that she'd have straight, out-of-the-eyes bangs. For an active ten-year-old, it had always been fine. And for her budding actress, Patricia's mother had wisely likened it to Bette Davis's hairstyle, which of course had more than satisfied Patricia at the time.

But now it just simply wouldn't do. So in true showstopping style, Patricia would drape a large bath towel over her head and flick it back and forth across her shoulders while she belted out "Gypsies, Tramps, and Thieves." With much aplomb and right in tune, Patricia did such a good rendition that you almost forgot she was just ten and was wearing a towel on her head.

Other people had noticed, too, and pretty soon Patricia started shedding her getups and singing at church—selected hymns, of course—and at school or anywhere anyone would let her. She even got the lead part in the annual school play. But after a time, performing skits at home, singing at church, and starring in school plays were not enough for Patricia. As she'd been saying forever and ever, she was going to the big city. And now, at ten years old, she was ready.

Of course her parents said, "No!"

"Dear Patricia," her mother said, "you've never even been away from home."

"You're still a little girl with a lot of growing and schooling to do," her father added. "It's a big world out there, and you'll have to be prepared. Tell you what: Keep on practicing, and if that's still what you really want to do when you're older, we'll talk about it then."

"I'm not a little girl, and I'll prove it," Patricia sobbed as she ran up the stairs.

She was going to do the most grown-up thing she could think of. So she went straight into her parents' bathroom, straight to the forbidden medicine cabinet, and straight to her mom's shiny silver razor. She was going to shave her legs. And before anyone could stop her, Patricia reached down and made one long razor stroke on each of her tender shins. But it didn't turn out how she thought. She didn't feel grown-up. She suddenly felt sick.

"I've killed myself!" Patricia screamed as she ran down the hall with deep cuts that were bleeding and stinging. She was headed straight for her mother, but she didn't make it. Around the curve, right before the top stair, she fell hard, and her ankle throbbed with pain. "I'm dying. I'm dying," Patricia screamed.

"All right, I'm coming, Patricia," her mother said as she mounted the staircase. "What's wrong now? You know you shouldn't pretend about things like that."

Patricia continued to sob, and as her mother slowly reached the top of the stairs, she saw the blood and realized that Patricia wasn't pretending this time. "Hurry!" her mother yelled to her father.

And before Patricia knew it, they were all in the car on the way to the hospital.

With the cuts on her shins bandaged and her broken ankle in a cast, Patricia returned home, sorry and tired. Thankfully she was going to be all right, but her parents still couldn't understand what had possessed Patricia to shave her legs, of all things.

"I just wanted to be grown-up so that you'd let me go to the big city," Patricia wailed.

"Oh, Patricia," her mother said. "Growing up isn't about any one thing a person does. It's lots and lots of experiences added together, day after day, that build an adult. And there will be more than enough time for you to follow your dreams, I promise. But now you'll need to take it easy. No acting or dancing skits for a while.

"Besides," she added as Patricia flopped into the big armchair, "it looks to me like you already have the best seat in the house."

Patricia just sighed. She didn't reply.

Sitting in her dad's easy chair, with a quilt over her lap and her foot propped up on an ottoman, Patricia looked every bit the ten-year-old that she was.

"This incident seems to have brought her back to her senses," her father whispered to her mother in the kitchen. "I think she might just forget about all this big-city dreaming for a while."

But they shouldn't have

spoken so soon. Hearing the front door open, they walked together into the den and saw Patricia hobbling out the front door.

"Patricia, where in the world do you think you're going?" her mother asked.

"Why, Auntie Em, I don't have the faintest idea of who you are talking about. But Toto and I have to get to Emerald City, so we're just going to follow the yellow brick road, follow the yellow brick road, follow, follow, follow . . ."

★　★　★

Trisha Yearwood grew up in Monticello, Georgia, where she was influenced by a variety of music at an early age. She learned country from her parents' record collection, rock and roll from the radio, and popular music from various choral groups and school musicals.

Trisha moved to Nashville in 1985 to attend Belmont University where she enrolled in the school's music business program. Shortly thereafter, she went to work as a receptionist in Nashville's recording industry district—called "Music Row"—and eventually found work as a demo singer, where she would sing songs on tape for writers who were trying to get their songs recorded. Ultimately, Trisha signed her own recording contract with MCA Records, and her very first tour was with fellow demo singer and friend Garth Brooks.

Trisha's first single, "She's in Love with the Boy," climbed to number one. Since then she has sold more than twelve million records, had ten number one singles, has been named both the Country Music Association's and the Academy of Country Music's Female Vocalist of the Year, and has won three GRAMMY Awards. In addition, she remains the only female country artist to reach platinum status or above on her first four album releases.

Trisha's appeal, however, has taken her beyond the boundaries of country music. She had a recurring role in the CBS series *JAG*, as well as appearances in numerous television specials. One of the personal highlights of her career was performing "The Flame" at the closing ceremony of the 1996 Summer Olympics in Atlanta.

Although she has lots of fond memories from her childhood, Trisha particularly remembers the pain and embarrassment of trying to shave her legs. Always acting out commercials and such, she says she just wanted to be grown-up. In addition, Cher was one of her favorite singers. Trisha says that she wanted more than anything in the world to be like Cher. It's suspected that with a towel on her head, and her voice, she probably came pretty close.

A Gift from the Angels

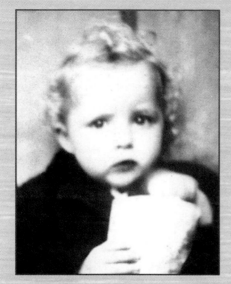

BRENDA LEE

Linda ran up and down the muddy banks of the creek. It would be dark soon, and she couldn't find Mae. "Mae," she yelled over and over again. "You come out right now!"

"Where is she?" Rick asked, running up, and out of breath. Ed, Charlotte, and Olivia were not far behind.

"Oh, she's just hiding somewhere," Linda said angrily. "But if she doesn't come out soon, Mama's gonna be mad at me for sure. I'm supposed to watch after her."

"Wait! I think I see her!" Charlotte yelled, pointing down at the creek.

And sure enough, as they all headed in that direction, Linda could see the top of Mae's head with her curly locks bobbing in the muddy water. Beside her on the bank was Ed's old red bicycle.

"Mae, are you all right?" Linda asked as she hurried down to her. "Give me your hand."

Mae stretched out her tiny hand, and with one good yank, Linda pulled her from the water. Mae was muddy from head to toe. The torn sash on her homemade dress dragged on the ground, and she was missing one of her new red cowboy boots. Otherwise, she seemed fine, and seeing that that was the case, Linda began to reprimand her. "What do you think you're doin'?" Linda scolded.

"Just swimmin'," Mae answered, as if nothing in the world was wrong.

"You can't swim in a muddy creek, Mae," Linda said, shaking her head back and forth and waving her finger from side to side. Mae imagined that if she didn't quit shaking so hard, her head would topple right off.

"And now you've gone and ruined your dress again. And for Pete's sake, where's your other boot?" Linda continued, still shaking her head from side to side with the other children peeking around from behind her.

"It's stuck in there," Mae said, pointing to the middle of the creek. "But, looky here, everybody. I found a little frog."

"Come on right now, Mae," Linda said. "And put that frog down. We gotta getcha cleaned up before Mama sees ya. And who knows what you're gonna tell Daddy about your boot."

"He won't be mad," Mae chirped. "He'll just get the angels to make me some more."

Linda rolled her eyes as Mae—still holding the frog—picked up the old red bike and started pushing it up the hill toward their house.

"Can I keep your bike a bit longer?" Mae asked Ed.

"Sure, Mae," he answered. "See ya tomorrow."

"Yeah, see ya tomorrow." Olivia, Charlotte, and Rick all waved as they headed across the muddy, red-clay backwoods to their respective houses for the night.

The Tarpleys' house was just over the hill from the creek, and Mae hummed as she walked while pushing the old red bicycle that was almost a head taller than she was. Like most all the other families around, the Tarpley family was dirt poor. They lived in a leaning, shotgun house that had only three rooms stuck together in a row, and an outdoor toilet. Their mama, Grayce, stayed at home to take care of the three children—Linda, Mae, and baby Randall—and their daddy, Ruben, found work as a carpenter when he could. More times than not, though, he was at home day after day. Mama would quietly explain to the children that Daddy was sick, but she and Linda knew otherwise. It was because of the whiskey jug that sat beside him on the front porch.

Today had been different, though. Daddy had gotten work somewhere, and as she and Mae trudged up the hill from the creek, Linda wondered when he'd be home and if he'd get some more work tomorrow. She'd heard Mama saying that they'd stretched the last job money about as far as it would go.

Thinking about these things, Linda glanced back at Mae, who was lagging behind, and said, "Mae, you just don't understand. Dresses are hard to come by, and so are boots."

Mae looked puzzled.

"Oh, never mind, you." Linda sighed. "You'll find out soon enough."

Of course Linda was talking about how hard their family had it, and because of it,

Linda seemed much older than her twelve years. But Mae was only six, and she hadn't yet noticed that the Tarpleys were poor. Mae believed she had everything she needed.

The old iron stove kept the house warm in the winter, and the creek kept everybody cool in the summer. The Tarpleys didn't own a car, but neither did most anybody else around them, and walking was more fun, anyway. Her grandmama Lucy Emma made all of her and Linda's dresses right out of flour sacks, and Mae thought they were some of the prettiest dresses around.

Besides that, there was always something good to eat. Mae didn't seem to notice or care that Mama cooked only rice and potatoes meal after meal, and she never found anything wrong with an occasional grease sandwich.

"Poor sweet Mae," Linda would say from time to time.

And still, Mae didn't understand the "poor" part. Besides a warm house, special-made clothes, and plenty of food, Mae also thought she had the best toys in town. Her daddy whittled one after another on the front porch next to the jug. There were always new batches of slingshots and little boats and tiny wooden people. Mae couldn't wait to get home today and see what new creation Daddy was going to make for her next.

"Daddy won't be home yet, Mae," Linda said as they were walking.

But when Linda and Mae come over the hill from the creek, their daddy was sitting on the front porch waiting. *The job must not have worked out this time*, Linda thought. Nevertheless, Ruben Tarpley looked as happy as always as he stood up and spread his arms wide toward them. "Well, here come my favorite two girls in the whole wide world," he hollered out to Linda and Mae. "Hurry up and give your daddy a big hug."

Mae dropped the old red bike and ran the rest of the way until she leaped into Daddy's arms. She was caked with mud and still wore the remaining red cowboy boot on her left foot.

"What do we have here, Booty Mae?" he asked, using his nickname for her. Nobody knew exactly why, but that's what he had called her since she was a baby.

Still holding the frog, Mae giggled. "Caught ya a frog, Daddy," she said, opening her hand wide and dropping the creature into the top pocket of his overalls.

"I see ya did. And I also see he must have given ya quite a fight," Daddy said, laughing.

"What's goin' on out here?" Mama asked as she walked outside and saw Mae. "Goodness gracious, child, what have ya done now, and where is your boot?" Mama asked, coming closer.

"I went swimmin', and it just got stuck in the mud. Just sucked right down," Mae answered.

"Well, Booty Mae, if that's the worst thing that happens today, then we'll all be just fine. I'll getcha some more boots," Daddy said.

"Ruben," Mama said, "ya know ya can't get any more boots for that child. I don't even know how ya got those. Lord knows we could have used the money."

"The angels made 'em, Mama," Mae said. "Daddy said so."

"Yep," Daddy said. "The angels made them for my angel. And they'll keep making things for ya, Booty Mae, because you're special."

"Oh, Ruben," Mama said, "stop that crazy talk right now or I'll throw that old jug so far, you'll never find it. Come on in, girls, and get cleaned up. Supper's 'bout ready."

That night, Mae climbed into the sagging single bed with Linda and baby Randall. She was glad that Daddy wasn't mad at her about the boot. She hadn't thought he would be. And she did believe that the angels would make her some more. The truth, of course, was that Daddy had saved money for the boots for a long time, but Mama could never figure out just how he'd managed to save it, much less where he'd hidden it. But just the same, Daddy had gone and bought Mae the pretty new red boots one day.

"A gift from the angels," he had announced to Mae, who had been so excited that she hardly took them off, not even when she slept.

But Mae was sleeping bootless tonight, and when she woke up, it was a breezy summer Sunday, and the Tarpleys started their early-morning walk to the church at the edge of town. Uncle Rob was the preacher, and all the relatives would be there to visit and pray and sing.

As the family marched reverently up the dirt road to the church, Mae started singing her favorite hymns. Every Sunday it was her voice that rang the loudest in the tiny country chapel. And even though you could barely see the top of her head over the worn wooden pews, you could always hear little Mae crystal clear with a voice bigger than anyone else's.

"It's the sweetest sound I'll ever hear—my Booty Mae singing to the angels," Daddy said as he shuffled along, beaming with pride.

Mae looked up and admired her daddy, who was holding her hand gently. He was scrubbed so clean that as the sun reflected on his forehead, Mae imagined he was wearing a shiny halo.

"Daddy," Mae said, "I don't think I want the angels to make me new boots."

"And why in the world would my little Booty Mae say that?" He looked down, smiling.

"I want a bicycle instead. One that I can ride," Mae answered.

"You have a bicycle, Mae. Or at least it's the same as being yours, seeing as though you've talked little Ed into letting you keep it most of the time," Mama said.

It was true. Ed's family was much better off than the Tarpleys, and he had gotten a new, bigger bicycle for his birthday. And even though Ed didn't actually give Mae his old one, he didn't mind if she borrowed it. The problem was that the bicycle was far too big for Mae to ride. She just pushed it, instead, everywhere she went.

When Mae's daddy heard her request, his brow wrinkled for a moment, and he looked far away down the road. Mama and Linda didn't say anything.

"Is that okay, Daddy?" Mae asked, interrupting the silence. "Will you get the angels to make me a bicycle instead?"

"Sure, I will, Booty Mae," Daddy answered. "But bicycles take a long time to make. It may be a while. Maybe as far away as your birthday."

Even though her birthday wasn't until late December, Mae said, "I'll wait, Daddy," as she squeezed his hand tight and skipped merrily next to him down the dirt road.

Carrying baby Randall on her hip, Mama looked silently ahead at the church steeple in the distance and prayed for an easier life.

★　★　★

Month after month went by, and the Tarpleys settled into fall. The hot, humid Georgia air was finally cooling down. Daddy hadn't found steady work since the summer, and times were particularly tight as little Mae continued to push Ed's old red bicycle around.

"Is my bicycle ready yet, Daddy?" Mae would ask every afternoon.

"Don't worry, Booty Mae," he said. "It's coming. It's gonna take just a little longer until your birthday."

Mama and Linda knew that the "little longer" was when Daddy found work, which probably wouldn't be until spring, when a lot of new construction projects would begin. It most certainly would be far past Mae's upcoming birthday. So it was a big surprise when Mae and Linda came home one crisp afternoon in late October and Daddy was at work.

"Daddy found a good job just right out of the blue," Mama said, looking relieved. "And the foreman said he would be working on it at least a month if he showed up regular."

"I don't want Daddy to leave," Mae said, stomping her foot. "I want him to stay here with me. What do you think, baby?"

Baby Randall sat in his diaper on a worn-out blanket in the middle of the floor. He wasn't old enough to know the difference about Daddy working one way or another. Mae looked at him for a moment, and when he didn't show any sign of answering her, she left in a huff to play outside. Mama's eyes trailed her out the door, and unlike Mae, she hoped that Daddy would keep the job.

Fortunately, Daddy did keep the job week after week. He brought money home to Mama every Friday, and it was always enough to make ends meet. Mama thought there might even be a little bit to save for Christmas if she was very careful with it. Her prayers for an easier life seemed to have been answered.

But the end of November came all too quickly, when a stranger arrived at the Tarpleys' door. He was a driving an old, battered pickup truck with lots of tools in the back and the biggest ladder Mae had ever seen. His overalls were dotted with paint, and he smelled of sawdust and whiskey. He introduced himself as Mr. Thomas.

"What brings you way out here to our house, Mr. Thomas?" Mama asked as she opened the door wider, with Linda and Mae beside her.

Mr. Thomas took off his paint-speckled hat and just stood there for a moment. Mama told Linda and Mae to scurry inside and stay there.

"Mrs. Tarpley," he began. "I'm sorry to bring ya some awful bad news."

Mama stood frozen, and her jaw tightened as she looked directly into the man's eyes. "What's happened to Ruben?" she asked.

"He's been in an accident, ma'am," Mr. Thomas said.

Mama didn't need to hear any more. She knew. As the man stood talking and saying how sorry he was, the words swam in Mama's mind. She stared over his right shoulder and looked down the dirt road. She would never see Ruben walking home again.

"And we don't know 'xactly how he fell off the ladder," the man was continuing. "But all of a sudden he did, and there wasn't a thing we could do. We tried, ma'am. We all tried. But there wasn't nothing nobody could do. I'm so sorry for you and the children. I'm so sorry," Mr. Thomas kept saying until he finally handed Mama a dirty, crumpled envelope containing Daddy's last work money.

"We took up a collection, so there's a little extra in there for ya, Mrs. Tarpley," he added.

"Thank ya, Mr. Thomas. God bless ya," Mama said as she took the envelope and slowly turned to go back inside.

"What's wrong, Mama?" Mae asked.

"Everything's gonna be all right, little Mae," Mama said as tears spilled silently down her weathered cheeks. "Run along and get your sister and tell her to come here to me. Then you go on outside and play until I call ya."

"Okay, Mama," Mae said.

Mama told Linda that Daddy had died, and Linda stayed inside for a long time. Then she came running out and down the dirt road without saying a word. Soon, she returned with Grandmama Lucy Emma and Uncle Rob, and they didn't come out, either, for a long, long time. Mae wondered what was happening, but she decided that Daddy would surely find out and tell her when he got home.

Finally, Mama called Mae inside and asked her to sit down. It was almost dark, and Daddy still wasn't there yet.

"What's wrong, Mama?" Mae asked. "When's Daddy gettin' home?"

"Be brave and listen to me, Mae," Mama said quietly. "Your daddy ain't coming home ever. He's gone to Heaven to live with the angels."

Mae sat very still for a moment and visualized Daddy living with the angels in Heaven. She imagined what a wonderful time he must be having, and then she understood. "I know why he went to Heaven," Mae said to Mama. "He's gonna help them make my bicycle for my birthday."

Mercy, Ruben, Mama thought. *Why would you promise the poor child such a thing?*

It was all so sad that Mama didn't know what to say. Mae would understand soon enough. Mama smiled, reached over and stroked Mae's curly locks, and said, "You're my angel now, Booty Mae." Just like Daddy would have done.

★　★　★

As Mae's birthday inched closer, it hadn't been hard to stretch the money that Mr. Thomas had given Mama. Since Daddy's fellow workers had all chipped in, there was a lot more in that envelope than she had expected. If Mama saved, she would have enough to last until January before she'd have to go work at the cotton mill.

But only a couple of weeks had passed when Mama announced that she had been to see the supervisor at the mill. She explained that she would have to start work the very next day. Linda was worried and confused. Only a few weeks before, Mama had insisted that they would have enough to make ends meet for quite some time.

"Daddy made some promises, and I've decided that it's best for all of us if I settle what he owes," Mama explained.

Linda sadly watched Mama rise early every morning, carry baby Randall to Grandmama Lucy Emma's, and then return late after a hard day's work. Mama never complained. In fact, she seemed strangely at peace as one chilly late-December morning arrived gloriously.

There was not a cloud in the sky as the sun warmed the shivering countryside. It was finally Mae's birthday, and the new red bicycle was waiting for her on the front porch.

"It's the prettiest bicycle I've ever had," Mae said, jumping up and down.

"Oh, Mama," Linda said, sighing, "how could you do such a thing? How will we ever get by now?"

Mama smiled as Mae rode her new gift around and around the dirt front yard, all the while singing to the angels at the top of her lungs. "Linda," Mama said, "it's taken me my whole life of living to understand your daddy, but now I do. Gifts from the angels are what help make life a lot easier. Why, just listen to Booty Mae. That's the sweetest sound I'll ever hear."

★　★　★

Brenda Lee—at a tiny four feet nine inches—stands tall in the music business. Known for her big voice, her vast roster of accomplishments, and a music catalog that spans rock and roll, R & B, pop, gospel, and country, Brenda has garnered worldwide record sales of more than one hundred million.

Discovered by Red Foley on the *Ozark Jubilee* national television show, Brenda began recording at age ten. She had her first hit record, "Sweet Nothin's," at age fourteen, which was closely followed by hit after hit, including "I'm Sorry," "Dynamite," "I Want to Be Wanted," "All Alone Am I," and the now-classic "Rockin' Around the Christmas Tree." In the pop field, Brenda enjoyed chart-topping success in the 1970s and earned a GRAMMY nomination for "Johnny One Time." Next came a slew of top ten country hits in the 1980s that included "Four Poster Bed" and "Tell Me What It's Like."

During her legendary career, Brenda has performed in some fifty-two foreign nations and has recorded international hits in Spanish, French, Japanese, German, Italian, and

Portuguese. Her list of awards and accomplishments spans decades and circles the globe, from appearing at a Royal Command Performance for Queen Elizabeth II to being inducted into the Country Music Hall of Fame. In addition, Brenda has been featured on several top movie sound tracks, including *Dick Tracy*, starring Warren Beatty, and *Only When I Laugh*, starring Marsha Mason; she appeared in *Smokey and the Bandit II* alongside Jackie Gleason and Burt Reynolds; and Brenda headlined the hit musical *Music, Music, Music* at Opryland USA.

The second daughter of Ruben and Grayce Tarpley, Brenda was born Brenda Mae Tarpley in the charity ward of an Atlanta hospital. Her father, a carpenter, was killed in a construction accident when Brenda was only eight years old. Brenda, however, fondly remembers her childhood and laughs when telling of losing her red cowboy boot, and pushing her friend's old bicycle everywhere she went. With a captivating wit, humble spirit, and incredible talent, Brenda remains one of the music business's most respected and well-loved entertainers.

Photo Credits